Ruffled Feath at Blackwaterfoot

Miller Caldwell

BeulAithris
Publishing

Scotland

First edition 2022

ISBN: 9798815993389

Dedicated

To my fellow Parkinson 's disease sufferers and to those who care for us.

The Reader's Bonus

To end this novella, I provide a selection of dreams that I have experienced, being one of only 5% of people in the country who can vividly recall dreams. Many are transported from my mind to my books. I hope you enjoy these short stories.

Finally, a poem, The Heron's Dream.

Contents

Chapter 1: No Hibernation

Blackwaterfoot on the west coast of the Isle of Arran, the kidney bean shaped island in the middle of the Clyde, has a summer visitor population over twice its normal size. By the last week in October, the village goes into partial hibernation. Clubs and activities continue but the visitors have all gone, left with happy memories. The community lingers on until the snowdrops sporadically appear, then the daffodils brighten up the verges and the villages prepare to welcome the return of relaxation-seeking visitors. Then, the new season has returned once more. That then, is the life of the village of Blackwaterfoot, in a nutshell.

This was not, however, the case in the year 2024. The village's feathers were about to be ruffled.

The Pan Am flight from JFK New York blazed its white trail over sleepy Arran on its way to Glasgow Airport. The event went practically unnoticed on the island beneath, except that its engines annoyed a collie on the beach, which looked to the sky, saw the vapour trail, and barked.

The plane began its descent through a crisp autumnal air over Greenock and Tony Lupino gave a sigh of relief. A sense of freedom, he felt. He took out his passport and gave it a satisfied look. He turned a page. There he saw the three-month tourist's visa to visit Britain, but he knew where he was going, he would not be leaving Scotland.

A Ford Kuga from the Arnold Clark stable of hired cars in Glasgow awaited him as he left the airport's forecourt. It suited his average frame, which had a mop of curly black hair on top of his head, while his skin seemed to sport a Mediterranean Italian tan. He checked his watch. 10:45 am. It left him ample time, to get down to the Ardrossan port with the aid of the car's Sat-Nav which fortunately understood his broad Nu Yok clipped accent.

The mid-week ferry sailing of the MV Caledonian Isles at 16:45, now on the winter sailing schedule, was boarded in good time. Tony went on deck to see Arran and marvelled at its near proximity. The Staten Island Ferry was the only sailing he had experienced before, and he did not have sea legs. Fortunately, the sea seemed calm that late afternoon. Only a quiver of waves responded to a faint breeze blowing towards the shore.

'Bit late for a holiday,' said a local Arran man in his early seventies with a smile and in need of a chat.

Tony looked at him with a puzzled grin. 'Just the break I need.'

'Are you coming for a week or longer?' he asked in a nonchalant manner.

'I guess if I like the place, I might stay awhile,' Tony replied feeling his non-committal to exactitude seemed appropriate, for the time being.

The man laughed. 'I've not met anyone who did not like Arran. So, what's your business, can I ask?'

Tony took a lengthy sigh. It was not a lie in his mind, more an indication he had a private life to maintain. 'Research,' he finally told him.

'Ah research,' the man nodded his apparent understanding. 'A big field is research.'

'Yeah, a big field,' Tony reiterated moving away to look over the port rails. The man followed him.

'What's that big rock?' asked Tony pointing in the distance, to the south side of the island.

'That's Ailsa Craig.'

'Inhabited?'

'Ah no,' he laughed loudly. 'Mind you there's no a curling stone in the land not hewn from its granite.'

Tony smiled and nodded his head. 'Now curling, I've heard of that. We've got that in Queens, Nu Yok, I guess.'

'Ah but your stone. It'll no be like oors. Only the blue hone has a very low water absorption rate, which prevents the action of repeatedly freezing water from eroding the stone's base.'

Tony glanced at the man. 'You know about curling then?'

The man nodded. 'I played at the Galleon Centre in Kilmarnock for many a year, in ma younger days.'

'But you live on Arran now?' Tony asked to clarify his reason for passage.

'Aye, I'm retired. I live at Lamlash,' he said looking towards the island in a moment of satisfaction. Then he thought they might meet again. 'You'll visit it, I'm sure. Is it Brodick you are bound for, yes?'

'Brodick? No, I'm headed for Blackwaterfoot.

Chapter 2: Alban Blackwater

The Best Western Kinloch Hotel at Blackwaterfoot opened its doors to Tony after he had parked in the car park at the front and arrived at the reception desk.

'Greetings, Mr Lupino. You must be tired after a long flight,' said Robbie Crawford the hotel manager, wearing a smile as wide as the Kilbrannan Sound and a lavender Pringle jersey.

Tony took a deep breath before replying. 'Yup I sure guess so. I don't sleep much on planes. I plan to catch some snooze and then be down for an evenin' meal. Is that in order?'

'It certainly is Mr Lupino. Your table will be reserved.'

'And...eh... dress code for the evening meal?' he enquired.

Robbie shook his head and smiled. 'Don't you worry about that, sir. Casual smart is the by-word,' reassured Robbie replacing a pen behind his right ear.

'Then casual smart it is.'

Tony's cases were taken by a staff member as Robbie gave Tony the key to room number 7.

After they entered, a handsome tip was given to the bag handler whose eyes widened as his open hand received a five-pound note. Tony kicked off his shoes, closed the curtains after gazing out of the window onto the Mull of Kintyre, put his jacket over a chair, flopped onto the bed and moments later he was snoring at a regular rhythm, in the land of nod.

He stirred about 6 pm, stretched, then made for the shower. It was there, as the flow of warm water and studs of creamy soap ran down his body, that he relaxed. New York was far behind him, and he had settled in the sleepy island community, where he felt confident his plan would unfold without a hitch.

He dried himself and sprinkled talc over his body. Then he opened his second case and took out his feather headdress. He laid it down on the bed, recognising the colourful feathers went well with the décor of the bedspread and with the ambiance of the room. He removed his moccasin shoes from his case and donned his traditional pants. He looked in the mirror. He smiled. The day he had planned, four months ago, was materialising. He took a deep breath. It calmed his racing heartbeat. The mirror smiled back at him. His confidence knew no bounds.

From his hand luggage he took out a small olive green-leather bag and squeezed it. He smiled. He opened his bedside table drawer and removed the Gideon Bible. He placed the bag at the back of the drawer then returned the bible to its rightful place. He felt sure it would be safe there, hid from any possible domestic staff's prying eyes.

He sat down in front of the mirror and from a small tartan tin containing crimson coloured clay, he dabbed lines of warrior red paint on his cheeks. The preparation was almost ready. Finally, he set his headdress in place, nestling in his rich black hair. He posed a solemn look at himself once more in the mirror. Yes, he was ready to dine.

He opened the door of his bedroom as a young child was passing. The girl gasped. She put her fist in her mouth and walked by slowly not taking her eyes off the unusual vision. Tony smiled at her and gave her a casual wave.

As Tony entered the dining room, the voices of all seven occupied tables came to a sudden halt. Silent mouths remained open, like landed fish, as their eyes met this unusual image.

Tony raised his hand. 'I bring you greetings from the great Sioux Nation. I shall, if you like, tell you why I am here when we finish our meal and retire to the lounge. May I invite you to join me then?'

Heads nodded in expectation. It was a very surreal moment for each diner, but the evening promised much and something not to be missed.

'We'd be delighted to hear your story, sir.' The man at table 2 said and then turned to his wife, pleased to have addressed a Native American Sioux chief.

'I'll set up the lounge,' said manager Robbie. 'I'm sure some of our own staff would be interested to hear about your life, or perhaps your double life, Mr Lupino,' he remarked causing diners to think the manger knew what seemed to be afoot.

Tony nodded then sat at his designated table by the window. It was dark outside, save for a light or two on far-away Kintyre, as the patter of rain showers beat a steady rhythm on the windows. The water then flowed in a wayward silent descent to the frame beneath.

Tony tucked into his T-Bone steak. Meanwhile Robbie turned up the temperature switch in the lounge. He also summoned Jeff and Ian to get ready to serve from the bar. Robbie wanted to set the scene for what promised to be a remarkable evening.

One hour and three quarters later, Robbie noticed the guests' plates and cutlery were at rest and suggested coffees and teas would be served in the lounge, where the bar would remain open.

'Thanks kindly, sir. It just has to be a Scotch on the rocks for me,' said Tony presuming his drink would be totted up on his final bill.

'Straight from the Lagg distillery, it's just down the road from here. The Arran Malt whisky it is, and with ice,' Robbie informed his Native American guest.

Tony waited till all the guests and some staff had settled down in a semi-circle in the spacious lounge. As they sipped their hot drinks and swirled their tongues around their mouths with their alcoholic preferences, Tony began to murmur. His gravelly voice increased, and the audience grew quieter.

'Hmmmmm....mmmmmm...mmmmm I am calling up the spirit of Alban Caskie...are you there Alban?.......yes...yes.... he's joining us.'

Tony's audience looked at each other fearing a journey into the dark underworld had begun. However, Tony immediately snapped out of his trance.

'Alban Caskie. Mark you well his name. Alban came from Blackwaterfoot. Yes, Bun na Dubh Abhainn, the Gaelic meaning bottom of the black river, as you know. He left this village under a cloud. It was said he had impregnated the laird's daughter. Never proved mind you, but that was the allegation. It was the year 1702. He left his family and the village and made his way through England to Bristol. From there he crossed the Atlantic.'

His audience was already spellbound in history. Their eyes focussed on the storyteller while their coffees and glasses were suspended mid-air, holding on to every word.

Tony continued. 'I believe he sailed on the clipper Foxglove. A supply ship sailing with victuals for the English troops in Massachusetts engaged in Queen Anne's War (1702-1713). He jumped ship in Boston and made his living selling corn in the summer in villages, and he was a skilled leather tradesman too. He travelled with his skills, as he trekked westwards all the while. He was a good hunter. Skills he learned in the Arran glens, I am sure. My people came across him on his journey and were satisfied he was no foreign spy but when he told us he was from Blackwaterfoot, it meant a lot to us. So, Alban Caskie joined the great Sioux clan and became in time, some seventeen years later, Chief Alban Blackwater.'

'Well, I never. I've never heard of a local becoming an American Indian, let alone an Indian chief,' said Robbie and heads nodded in agreement.

'No, that's because there were no journalists following him. But in the New World, Alban had found his roots; and made a new beginning. In time he married a Sioux girl and if you follow that line of descent down six generations, you come to well, you come to me. I am the descendant of Alban Caskie, Chief Blackwater. And I believe I am the first of Alban's descendants to land on Alban's island home, here at Blackwaterfoot.'

The gasps were drowned by a round of applause and Tony enjoyed their reaction, shown in his broad smile.

'So, is this a pilgrimage you are having or just a holiday?' asked Neil, a wealthy local diner.

'A good question. In fact, I think I might put some of my traditional Red Indian powers to good use. I can water divine,' Tony said with a grin of satisfaction.

A round of laughing ensued. 'So, can I. We don't need any rain assistance here. Just look outside right now,' said Neil pointing to the running raindrops continuing to meander down the windowpane.

'Oh no, no, of course, not just finding rainwater. I can find rare minerals too. I use a secret Sioux skill for that.'

'So, you will be prospecting for gold perhaps in the Arran hills? Just like many have done before you and found nothing,' added Neil.

'No, no that's not true, gold has been found in wee bits in 2001 and 2006 in Argyll, no far fae here,' said loyal Kinloch drinker, Eric.

'I'm not surprised sir; it is what I may find out, using my own Sioux skills, as I said.'

'And how long will it take you?' asked Ann, Neil's wife.

'How long is a shark's tooth, a piece of string, or a winter's night? I may be here till Christmas.'

'Then you'll be one of us by then Tony, I mean Chief Blackwater. In fact, what do you wish us to call you?'

'I'm Tony. I work in Nu Yok as a lawyer,' he told them. 'Dat brings in de beans. But I always wanted to get back to my ancestor's country, now that my wife Ella, Princess Blackwater, has died.'

His audience grew quiet for a solemn moment as they absorbed Tony's sad announcement.

'Minnesota is where Alban Caskie is buried, in a Sioux burial ground. He's there and I'm here where he grew up. It's a powerful feeling folks. I'm sure pleased to be with you all this evening. And I sure appreciate you hearin' me out.'

Robbie stood up and led the applause. 'Not often do we have such a celebrity in our midst. Give our guest a hand,' he said, and all stood to thank Tony for his family history lesson, with enthusiastic clapping. Tony lifted his glass, threw back his head and then placed his empty whisky glass on the table. He relaxed. His plan was working well. He had the community on his side.

Chapter 3: Well Tony, An Interesting Day?

The following day was dull. Very dreary indeed as any outside vision was curtailed by grey mist. The line between land and sea was indistinguishable. That suited Tony. He welcomed the shroud of secrecy.

After a hearty cooked breakfast, Tony returned to his room and consulted a booklet entitled Arran – 40 Favourite Walks. He studied the literature carefully and settled on page 36. Loch Tanna.

But first he struggled into his waterproofs then he opened his bedside drawer to retrieve his green bag. He placed it in his hip-pocket and zipped it close.

The weather was improving slightly as he drove out of the car park and set off north to Catacol Bay. It took twenty leisurely minutes in his Ford Kuga till he arrived at the Catacol Bay Hotel car park, at the north-west end of the island.

The rain had stopped; the sky was less densely clouded. Some blue sky was peeking through. Tony had enough time for a black coffee.

'Whit nae milk or sugar?' asked the waitress with the disgusted face of a cat drinking sour milk.

'No Ma'am, just pure coffee.'

'American, are ye?'

'Guess you can tell from the accent. Yeah, Nu Yok born and bred.'

The waitress was still sizing up the American. 'So, whit ye daein' oan Arran?'

'Let me tell you, I'm sure one of your folk. My ancestor came from Blackwaterfoot,' Tony said with an air of satisfaction.

The waitress screwed up her face. 'Yer ancestors? Nae ancestor o' mine. I came fae Glesca twa year ago.'

'So, you are not an Arran native?'

'Nah.'

'So why are you here now?' he asked out of interest.

'Here's yer coffee. Ask nae questions; git nae lies.'

Tony drank his coffee in silence. He smiled as he recalled he had at last met the proverbial dour Scot. Before leaving he had a final request. He approached the waitress, with a degree of reservation.

'Can I, ...er leave my car here while I go for a walk?'

'Aye, ye can leave it a' day long. It micht gie me mair business.'

Tony was pleased the rain had ceased. He was able to consult his booklet in the open. He walked along the road south and reached a road bridge before a large white house. It was named Fairhaven. Its name promised some good luck, in his mind. He needed just that. He found the signpost 'Glann Dimhan and Loch Tanna.' The path followed the river Abhainn Mòr over rocky outcrops and heather-coated knolls. Tony put down his rucksack and unzipped his back pocket. He bent down as if to wash his face in the running water but instead opened his green bag and took out two small nuggets of gold and placed them behind a stone and secured it in its watery position. Satisfied with his work, he continued his way noticing the water flow over vast granite slabs, which formed minor waterfalls. He eased himself down one such feature and followed its course into a rushing stream where he again hid two more gems. Four bean-sized nuggets of gold were secured. A fifth nugget was laid further downstream. Five gold nuggets were now in position. The sixth and final nugget remained in his tartan purse and settled back in his zipped rear trouser pocket. He stood up and smiled at the sky. He had achieved what he had planned in New York and now completed on Arran. He felt good.

Loch Tanna appeared in due course and Tony made for its sandy shore. He trod on the sand. The sun came out and warmed his skin. He could not resist the opportunity. He looked around. He was very alone. He stripped naked and entered the loch. He swam on his back and looked up at the increasingly blue sky. He gasped as the cold water and his temperature fought for compatibility. Yet the freshness was such a contrast to the busy automobile air-clogging New York streets. Such solitude. Only the trill of a small unseen bird was heard. His thoughts did not linger. Such an opportunity had been achieved but his limbs were starting to ache with the coldness encompassing his body. He made his way to the shore. He shook himself dry as the gentle wind assisted the process.

The invigorated Tony made his way back, tracing every step of the way, returning to where the gold nugget drops had been laid. He was as satisfied as a hunter, having set traps down in position.

Autumn daylight was fading slightly as he returned to the hotel. Robbie Crawford was behind the reception desk when he arrived back.

'Not the best of Arran days, Tony. Bad start to the day. You can't expect much warmth these days, now October has arrived.'

Tony stood in front of Robbie. He looked straight into his eyes. 'Not the best of Arran days, you say. I could not disagree with you more. It's been a marvellous day. I managed a swim too. But come over here. I've got something to show you,' he said with a wink in his eye.

Robbie pondered his expression. Then he made his way over to the lounge looking perplexed as Tony relaxed in a leather chair beside a low coffee table.

Tony put his hand in his pocket and brought out a blue coloured handkerchief. He cupped his hand. Then he held a corner of his handkerchief. He shook it. On to the coffee table dropped a small nugget of gold.

Robbie sat back in astonishment. He looked at the gleaming gem. He bent forward. He lifted it up.

'Clean as a whistle. Surely not pure gold is it?'

'It's pure, most certain. It's Arran gold.'

Robbie's mouth was ajar, unable to find the right words.

'Washed from the granite stones in the north end of the island,' Tony added.

'And with Sioux utterings the gold appeared?' asked Robbie recalling last night's discussion.

'Yes, exactly. Sacred Sioux sayings and a keen eye took me to the gold.'

'But where did you find the gold? Will there be more?'

'Oh yes, there could be more but the location, I cannot say just yet.'

'You are keeping it a secret?'

Tony seemed to suck an invisible sherbet lemon. 'You know, you are the only one who knows I've located gold?'

'I presume so.'

'Let's keep it that way for the time being. And this nugget, it's yours to have.'

Robbie's mouth opened wide. He glared at the gold once more. 'You are giving me a gold nugget?'

'Why not? When further gold is found, you can say you were first to be in the know.'

'I can't thank you enough. Can I ask you what its value might be, for a nugget this size?'

'You mean in money terms?'

'Yes.'

'Well now Robbie, by the time you find more nuggets, you might want to make some jewellery for your wife. Not so?'

'That's an idea.'

'Then best not tell her of your good fortune for the time being.'

'But gold, should I not tell the authorities? I don't want to commit a crime.'

Tony gulped. 'That's your legislation, is it?'

'Well yes. It has to be reported if it's found.'

'I see,' said a puzzled Tony. He looked at the ceiling momentarily. 'Finders keepers, in America.'

The following day Tony returned to Loch Tanna to inspect his gold drops. All were all in place and would be easily found once the gold-diggers were informed of where the gold was located. He was pleased. They would be safe for the time being. Few would venture up this way in late October, without good reason. He left the gems behind and decided to walk inwards towards Beinn Nuis at a summit of 2,597feet.

He had a knapsack containing the hotel's sandwiches and he sat down on a turf to eat his lunch. It was as he ate, his eye caught a flicker in the sky. He stopped eating and looked upwards. Beyond doubt he was seeing the wingspan of the Golden Eagle. He watched it soar heavenward then drift in a circle downwards. He rummaged in his knapsack for his phone then he switched it on. His camera struggled to find the eagle. Then Tony switched his video camera on. The bird dived towards the ground, stopping briefly before rising up with a rabbit in its gigantic powerful claws. His photos would eventually be recorded for posterity in his New York apartment. As the bird flew off, as a speck in the sky, he played back his video recording. He was amazed to have the bird in focus and in its hunting mode. He would treasure those shots.

After eating his apple and drinking his orange juice, he threw away the biodegradable core and he resumed his way noticing the ground rise with each step. To his right however he noticed a disfigurement of the land. Quite a large area, the length of three Buick automobiles perhaps, he thought. He made his way towards it, focussing in a concentrating manner, trying to decide what it could possibly be.

The raised land seemed to cover a wider piece of ground as he came nearer. It was like a cross. The wind got up and whistled around him, as he approached. He wondered if wind and rain was beginning to unearth this strange shape. The ground was soft and his foot occasionally sank into soggy marsh. His sock absorbed the water. But he was determined to understand what he was seeing.

Then he realised a wing was becoming visible. He scraped away the earth and grass and then there was little doubt what he had discovered. It bore olive green camouflaged metal and a partly hidden swastika was unmistakable. It was clearly not a recent crash. Tony realised it must have been a WW II aircraft which would have hit the higher ground on the far right and its velocity had brought it to a rest where it was now emerging.

He dug away with his hands, bending a nail backwards in a moment of extreme shock and pain. Yet, in reality, he made little impact in uncovering the metallic monster. However, beyond doubt, he had cleared enough grass and lichen to show it was a stricken aircraft. He took several photos with his phone camera. He looked around to see if anyone was in the vicinity.

The area was very desolate. Only the wind around his ears made any sound at first. But the sweet trill of a lark on high was heard and in the distance a trickle of water was occasionally in his earshot. That stream trickled towards the waterfall where his gold remained hidden.

He retraced his steps and was eventually at the main road where he had left his car. As he drove back to Blackwaterfoot, he wondered just what would be the outcome of his uncovered plane. Would he have any right of ownership? Could he be interviewed at a price? Would eyes be on the stricken plane but also in the streams? These thoughts continued until he arrived back at the hotel.

Robbie was seated doing some accounts at a desk when he arrived. He looked up. 'Well Tony, an interesting day?'

Tony sauntered over to where Robbie was working. 'Better leave you to your work. I'll tell you later.'

'I won't be long. Can I get you a coffee?'

'That's swell, sure thing.'

'Black, no milk or sugar?' Robbie confirmed as he lifted the phone and passed on the order to the kitchen.

Tony sat in what was becoming his usual leather chair by the window. The day had brightened, and the village of Carradale on Kintyre seemed to be in his line of sight.

Then he took out his phone and scrolled through his photos. When he got to the plane's best picture, he enlarged the shot with his index finger and thumb. It looked sharper than he had seen before. There was no doubt what he had uncovered.

Robbie arrived with two coffees. He handed a cup over to Tony.

'Well, what did your Sioux utterings discover today,' laughed Robbie but Tony's face looked solemn.

'Ah yes, the Sioux spell worked wonders,' he said handing over the phone to Robbie.

Robbie took the phone and turned it round. He strained his eyes to make sense at first at what he was seeing.

'Did...you take this...this photo today?'

'Yes, all five of them.'

Robbie scrolled through all the photos. 'You mean you discovered a plane?'

'Yeah, it looks like a WWII Nazi plane.'

Robbie looked at Tony, his eyebrows gathered together.

'Sioux magic again?'

'Yeah, seems so. What do I do now?'

'Where did you find the plane?'

Tony consulted his booklet. 'Here,' he pointed with his finger. 'Just below Beinn Nuis.'

Robbie took the booklet and studied it. 'Good heavens. What the heck were you doing up there? It's the middle of nowhere, almost in the middle of winter.'

'It's where the spirit of the Sioux led me. I can't say much more...... I can actually. Here, let me find it.'

Tony brought up the Golden eagle video with its catch and showed it to Robbie.

Robbie drew the screen closer to his eyes. He shaded his eyes with his hand. 'That's stunning. This should be in a nature magazine. Actually, we might call that the luck of the Irish, but the Sioux seems to have a keener knowledge of our part of the island.'

'I'm not an ornithologist. None of our family are. We're all city folk. Just lucky I was there.'

'Well,' said Robbie scratching his head. 'It's not the first Golden eagle found on the island, but this WW2 plane crash is an amazing discovery. Last one was one of ours. But there's not been a plane crash here for a very long time, and I don't recall a German one. We've got to report this finding. I'll phone Rory Murdoch.'

'Rory Murdoch? Who is he?'

'Sergeant Murdoch is our local policeman. At least he should be in the know.'

'The police?'

'Oh yes, Tony. They'll have to secure the site. After all, it will be a sacred burial spot.'

'I guess so. Yup, it is that.'

Robbie retired to his home quarters and lifted the phone. Rory had just finished a mug of his favourite Guatemalan coffee when the call came through.

'Good evening, how can Police Scotland help you?'

'Hi Rory, Robbie Crawford in Blackwaterfoot here.'

'Oh yes, Robbie. What can I do for you?'

'Well, a few things don't seem quite right. Hard to put a finger on it, mind you.'

Rory drummed a pen on his desk. 'Go for it. I'll soon see where the crime element comes in.'

Robbie told Rory about his unusual Sioux guest and his methods in finding gold and a German plane.

'What on Arran?' exclaimed Rory in a shout through the open window which disturbed some roof-top crows.

'Yes, he's a bit of a bombshell in the village. Everyone seems to be talking about him,' said Robbie retrieving a handkerchief and giving his nose a clearing. 'And he gave me a gold nugget.'

'A gold nugget? What? Okay, you did right by telling me of it. Mind you I can't see any offence he's caused. He says he's found gold. Okay, that's still to be confirmed. But this aircraft he's found. I'd better get the area sealed off before it becomes a visitor attraction. Give me more time to think about that gold. Good heavens gold! You've certainly given me some work here.'

Chapter 4: Where Can Callum Be?

DI Alan Dunbar, Rory's mainland boss, was advised of the discoveries and arranged for a mainland contingent to have a vigil in place before excavation of the plane. Alan also informed the Geology and Archaeology departments at Glasgow University of the gold findings and the Nazi airplane on Arran and that created an interest group of final year students who made for the island, a day before the weekend. But an embargo holding back the news about a gold field was to be maintained for the present and Alan insisted the University did not breach that trust.

DI Dunbar realised he needed more specific information and phoned Rory as he ate a digestive biscuit and occasionally dunked it into his cooling Guatemalan coffee.

'Hi Rory. I didn't get the location of the gold,' admitted the DI.

Rory felt a reprimand coming. 'I haven't got it, yet either.'

'Well, find out and let me know as soon as you do.'

'Okay but Robbie Crawford, the hotel manager doesn't know where his gold came from either.'

There was a moment's hesitation. Minds were working overtime.

'Rory, I think you had better meet this American. Put some pressure on him to reveal where the gold is.'

'Yes, sir. That was on my mind too,' he said feeling his response hit the mark.

Rory set off to the hotel, going around the south tip of the island, wondering just what the American was doing in Blackwaterfoot out of season. His mind was preoccupied with meeting this unusual visitor to the island. Would he be in Native American attire or more relaxed on his holiday. He had not even recalled ever speaking to a New Yorker before. There were sure to be some cultural differences, as an episode of Cagney and Lacey came to mind. As the police car passed the Lagg distillery on the southwest side of the island, his car phone pinged. His hand-free set was turned on and he acknowledged the distressed caller. He knew her. She was from a hamlet near his base in Lamlash.

'Please help me, Rory. Jean Dalrymple here. It's Callum. He has not returned home. I last saw him yesterday morning and he's never been home since. It's not like him. I'm really worried.'

'Remind me Jean. How old is Callum?' asked Rory.

'He's seventeen next month,' Jean said holding her fleshy throat with her fingers as she spoke.

'Has he a girlfriend?' queried Rory.

'A girlfriend? No, not to my knowledge. I'm sure he would have told me if he had.'

'Okay, I'm in my car at present on my way to solve another case, so I'll pass on your concerns to PC Colin Cole back at the office. He'll make enquiries. I'll be back to him later this afternoon. Do let us know if Callum turns up. Like lost dogs they often do, Jean,' he said to give her some hope.

Rory phoned Colin and appraised him with Jean's concerns. He told him to check with his school friends and then the ferry sailings. But Rory wanted to get to the enigmatic American. He resumed driving on to Blackwaterfoot.

Rory entered the hotel and was met by Robbie.

'That Guatemalan coffee I smell?' asked Rory with a sniff of the air.

'I suspect, if I am not mistaken, it's a Columbian one. You don't mind?'

'No, any coffee makes me concentrate better. So, is Tony Lupino in? Can he join us?'

'He's not far away. On the beach just now but he'll be back soon. His car is still here.'

Rory took a seat and brought out his police notebook. 'Has he told you where he found the gold yet?'

'No, he hasn't. Mind you I've only asked him once and that was a couple of days ago.'

Rory pouted his lips and nodded his head. 'I see,' was all he said. Then his eyes lit up.

'Ah the coffees.'

Having finished their coffees, Robbie looked through the hotel window and made an announcement.

'Here's the man himself, the Sioux Chief, or perhaps I had better introduce him as he introduced himself when he arrived.'

Robbie went over to the door and opened it for Tony.

'Hi Tony. Come meet my friend Rory,' he said ushering him into the room. 'I've some work to do. I'll be in the office if you need me,' said Robbie turning away with a smile.

'Hello Mr Lupino. We don't get many visitors on Arran at the end of October. A special visitor too. Good to see you, sir.'

'Good day officer. You say a special visitor? What do you mean, exactly,' said a very reserved Tony.

Rory thought quickly without looking concerned. 'Well, I hear you are a descendant of a local Arran man, is that not so?'

Tony relaxed on familiar territory. 'Yup that's a fact. I am a direct descendant of Arran's own Alban Caskie, Chief Blackwater. I am the Sioux's present incumbent.'

Rory nodded his understanding. 'So, you are also a Sioux chief?'

'Yes, Blackwater is a subsection of the great Sioux Nation.'

'And er... your methods...your special powers...your er...'

'Probably magic to you. Perhaps it's like your Highlander's special powers of insight.'

'Yes, there's something in that but you are particularly successful. After all, you have found gold and a WW II German plane. That's quite an achievement for someone not from the island. You surely agree?'

'Many Nu Yokers don't climb the Empire State building. Not many locals go into the hills, I do. It's where I am at peace with the spirits of the Sioux. So different from downtown Nu Yok.'

Rory nodded in agreement then he crossed his legs. 'So, the spirit of the Sioux led you to find gold, as well?'

'Yes, I found some gold. There's probably more gold at the site but I'm not sure who owns the land. Soon be a need to stake the ground for a gold rush.'

'Depends on where the site is,' posed Rory. 'Even a vague indication where it is, would be helpful.'

Tony nodded as he thought through his reply. 'Gold is in the river, well, stream I suppose, at the waterfall on the Alt nan Calman on the way to Loch Tanna,' confirmed Tony to Rory who noted this in his silver notebook.

Rory nodded, like a donkey, as he wrote. Then he placed a line under his notes. He turned a fresh page. 'And the aircraft?'

Tony held nothing back now. 'I started off from Dougarie on the west coast and followed the river up Glen Lorsa. Then I was led towards Beinn Nuis and the land between that mountain and Beinn Tarsuinn. The plane lies between the two mountains. I guess it must have clipped the Tarsuinn Mountain and landed in the soft terrain.'

Rory scribbled away then put his pen top onto his biro.

'Well, regarding the land up there, it's the Dougarie Sporting Estate that owns the rights of the area around the Lorsa River that flows into the Loch Tanna. Forest and Land Scotland owns beyond the area. Contact them and I'm sure they would be delighted to hear of the gold. I've been on Arran all my life and to find gold, well, it's just not a daily occurrence, is it? In fact, just a little short of a miracle. As for the aircraft, that's just a remarkable find as well. The University of Glasgow will be on the island by the weekend and their excavation will commence before the year is out. I guess they will have they will have the gold to investigate too.'

Rory gathered his cap and notepad and stood up.

'Well, it's been a pleasure meeting you Chief Blackwater,' he said offering his hand. Tony shook his firmly in part because the officer had no other interest in him and that suited him fine.

'Now, I've another worrying case. Must be on my way. See you soon, Robbie,' he shouted through on his way out, to no response. And with a revving of his police car, Rory was off to the station at Lamlash once more.

Robbie returned to his guest. 'Tony, I guess we are all wondering about these Sioux powers you have. We are all probably a bit sceptic, you know....er...despite the gold find and the aircraft too. It's an uncanny duo, you've got to admit.'

Tony nodded. 'I guess I was brought up with the Sioux insight. That's all. Seeing things the Sioux way. Tell you what, tonight I'll give a show. How about that?'

'Another after dinner talk as it were?'

'Exactly,' Tony said giving Robbie a thud on his shoulder.

Colin and Rory sat in the police station mulling through the facts. Rory nursed yet another Guatemalan coffee, while Colin drank some Tetley tea.

'So, Colin, you are telling me there's no reason to suspect murder, yeah?'

PC Colin Cole shook his head. 'No. No body, reported.'

'That's a relief.'

'I did a search of the family house at Glenkiln. His bedroom was neat, nothing of interest there. Checked at the secondary school, too. His classmates both girls and boys had no inkling why he's missing. No known girlfriend either. One lad said his spotty face was not his best feature. His best friend is Michael McGregor. He told me he spoke to him the night before he went missing. Nothing was on his mind to suggest he'd vanish.'

'Ferry?' Rory fired at Colin.

'No, definitely not a passenger.'

'Access to a boat?'

'Unlikely. No, not a wealthy home. I informed Marine Scotland Police who can do a harbour check and they can sweep the coastline, to see if a body has been washed ashore. That's about it. Not much else we can go on at this stage. We need some sort of breakthrough.'

Rory stood up. He hitched his trousers up too. Then he looked straight at Colin.

'There's just one option left at this stage. Keep it secret for the time being. I don't want the mainland to know about this, yet.' Rory pushed some paper along his desk. He lifted the phone.

'Hi Robbie, is Tony there? I'd like a word with him.'

'He's in his room. I'll put you through.'

'Great.' Rory drummed his fingers on his desk. Colin was following the conversation and knew it centred on the Blackwaterfoot hotel.

'Hi Tony. All well?'

'Yes, sure is. Just polishing off an act I'll be giving tonight.'

'Wish I could be there.'

'All invited.'

'Thanks. It's business I want to discuss with you. We have a missing 16-year-old boy, a bright lad, almost 17.

Not a murder, just a complete disappearance. I was wondering...well.....you know.... …your Sioux insight... …if you could shed some light on the case?'

'Missing youth, male. Guess you've spoken to his girlfriend, his friends, was he depressed, hurt, done the usual tests and drawn a blank, eh?'

'He has no known girlfriend, that's it. No leads at all.'

Tony also learned where he lived. It was part of the island he did not know. 'Got any police tracer dogs? Get some of the boy's clothing for it to sniff and get a trail. That's how the Nu Yok police would do it at this stage of the enquiry.'

'You know about police work?' asked Rory in surprise.

'I am a Nu Yok District Attorney back home, a prosecuting attorney, if you will. No police reports; no work.'

'It is a mainland police dog we use. I'll get that arranged. I just thought with your special insight, you might er.......'

Tony cut in. 'Okay, I'll give it my best shot.'

Tony took out his map of Arran and studied it carefully. He drew a circle around a spot. He had a starting position identified.

That night, dressed in his traditional Red Indian Sioux outfit once more, the guests retired to the lounge where Tony held their attention.

'I have before me a pack of large cards. They are not traditional cards but have pictures on each one. Now who will pick a card?' He looked around the group and his eyes settled on one lady whose hand was starting to rise.

'Madam, may I ask you to come forward. You name please.'

'I'm Joan Linton, a resident of Blackwaterfoot.' Joan was lean, wearing a long green and yellow dress with brown heels on her feet. Her necklace was dated jewellery, probably an inherited item.

Tony shuffled the cards in front of her eyes. 'All the cards have traditional Sioux figures. Joan, select a card and look at it.'

Joan ran her fingers along the top of the cards, and she chose the penultimate one. She extracted the card and stared at it.

'Tell the audience which card it is.'

'It's a young Native American girl riding on a piebald horse.'

'You know the breeds of horses well, madam. Now show the card to the audience.'

'A horse rider. That tells me you are about to travel. I can't say when, maybe tomorrow maybe next week but travel is your theme. It can be different types of travel as well. A trip up the road to Lochranza or a trip further afield. I cannot tell you more, but you are definitely about to travel.' Tony ushered Joan back to her seat.

'Next volunteer. Now who wishes to select a card?' Tony ignored Joan's hand as she raised it again; she had had her turn.

'Excuse me, I have to tell you something, I forgot,' said an excited Joan. 'We sail on the ferry on Friday and take the train to Glasgow to visit our daughter in the city.

It's her birthday, 4th November. That's our travel arrangement. You got it right.'

The audience wowed and applauded, and a forest of hands went up once more. Tony saw Robbie raise his hand. He asked him to come forward and he confidently selected another card. He looked at it and informed the group that it was a large Native American family.

'In our culture a large family means prosperity. With more in the family, more income arrives. That creates wealth. It does not come overnight, you must wait but prosperity will come your way, Robbie. The Sioux have ordained that.'

'Very promising news Tony, I can't wait to see how my fortunes might change.'

'Are there more volunteers?' Tony asked as he scanned his audience.

'Hi I'm Stephen. I've been on the island for almost eighty-six years. I can't see a new wife coming my way. But I'll give it a go, I might be wrong. I might be lucky.'

The audience laughed sympathetically at his remark.

Stephen got up with the aid of his gnarly wooden stick. He moved like he might collapse at any moment, like a broken stepladder. His fingers loitered over the cards in a shaky movement. Stephen knew most present were aware of his Parkinson's disease. But he selected a card and told the group that there was a Native American woman at prayer as a black cloud made its wayward way heavenward in the sky.

Tony took the card and asked Stephen to return to his seat. 'This is a sombre moment. Someone you love has died and is at peace. The Native American lady is saying a traditional Sioux prayer to welcome the soul of the departed into the life ever after. All pain has gone and with a smile on her face, the departed makes her way to the Sioux kingdom of eternal peace.'

The atmosphere was solemn. All eyes were on Stephen. Would he take his final breath in their presence?

The telephone rang at the reception. Robbie set off to answer it.

Meanwhile Tony gathered his cards and put them on the table and sat down. 'Perhaps you might like to know how I manage two lives; one in Nu Yok and one in Minnesota?'

From the reception area, Robbie called out. 'Stephen, a call for you. It's your son.'

Robbie held the phone as Stephen made his way slowly to it as Tony began to tell the group about his birth in New York.

'Yes, at last. I expected it,' shouted Stephen. 'When? Okay, I'll let you make the arrangements. Yes, tomorrow, that's fine. Till then... Bye.'

Stephen made his way back to the group with the widest of smiles. All studied his face. Surely, he would share his apparent good news?

'Well, there's a new person on Arran who is the oldest on the island. My mother has died aged 108. It's less of a death. It's more of a celebration of a long and happy life.'

And all agreed.

Chapter 5: Callum is Found

Tony drove south and took the Ross Road across the southern island and parked at a picnic table just a little over halfway across the island. He had not met even one vehicle on the road. The solitude sharpened his sinews as he strode southward until he reached the Squiler Burn. A curlew sang its plaintive call urging him on. He stood and watched its flight. Then a vulture of some kind, perhaps a sparrow hawk or a maybe a kestrel flew above to see his progress, but he knew Scottish wildlife was not Sioux fauna, nor was the Minnesota flora the same in Scotland.

The wind increased as he lengthened his step. He knew where he was heading, and it took him the best part of an hour before the Urie Loch began to appear. He stopped to admire its dark brooding water and he looked along the grass beside the loch. Only one spot, almost out of sight, caught his attention.

He continued by the Squiler burn wondering if trout were hiding from his footsteps. They were safe that day, Tony had no rod. The loch was no more than 500 yards away and he knew this was the best chance he had to find Callum Dalrymple.

He reached the grassy lip and discovered clothing, male clothing. He came across trainers with socks tucked neatly inside. It seemed Callum had taken to the water when a bolt of autumn sunshine came his way. Tony stared at the loch. He had swum recently too. Of course, Tony had no idea what time of day he had entered the water. It was a sobering thought. Water and its attractions were universal. The loch shimmered in the breeze. He would not venture into the water and befall a similar fate, but he felt he had the proof that his body must be in Urie Loch. His mobile rang the police at Lamlash.

'Hi, can I speak to Sergeant Rory Murdoch, please.'

'Who is calling?'

'Tony Lupino.'

'One moment please Mr Lupino.'

Tony drummed his fingers on his trouser leg.

'Hello Sergeant Murdoch, can you hear me? The line seems to be cracking. I've found clothing. I guess it's Callum's.'

'Where?'

'At Loch Urie. I feel he went swimming and got into difficulty.'

'And where are you?'

'I'm at the loch.'

'Well, it will take some time to get this underway. I need a boat, cadaver dog, and additional staff. Could be the best part of two hours. You'll still be there?'

'My car is on the Ross road at a picnic table. That's where I'll go after we meet up,' said Tony straining to hear Rory speak.

'Okay we'll get you back to your car, eventually. Can you hold on?'

'What did you say?' asked Tony with a screwed-up face facing into the breeze.

'Stay where you are. We'll be on our way.'

As Tony switched off his mobile phone he wondered if Rory had got his position correct and if he had conveyed the solemn message adequately. He stood up and took a deep sigh. He felt he had done enough but had to stay. He sat down and opened his phone again. He entered Solitaire as such games evaporated time, at a good rate.

The only diversion from his game was a hare he saw bounding over the land and the song of a lark high in the sky, which the sun prevented Tony seeing. Not long after, the sun dropped lower, and he wondered if Rory might still arrive in daylight.

The light faded as he heard a humming noise grow louder. He searched for its source and eventually saw the rotating wings of a helicopter approach. He stood up and waved at the mechanical bird and its headlights seemed to flicker its response.

The helicopter's noise shattered the peaceful silence and as it landed, a dog appeared jumping out before the craft settled on land and immediately sniffed the vicinity, planting its scent. Tony recognised Rory in his Police no 2 uniform and they shook hands.

'Getting late, you'll have to put the search off till tomorrow,' said Tony assessing Rory's restricted options.

At that moment from the silent helicopter the pilot took out a rubber tube and began to pump air into it. A boat appeared from his efforts.

'So where is Callum's clothing?'

'Over here, Rory,' said Tony taking him to the grassy knoll.

'Patch, come here. Good boy.' Rory took some of the clothing and rubbed it against Patch's snout. 'Go seek, Patch, go seek.'

No sooner had the instruction been given, than Patch bounded into the water and began to swim. The inflated boat made its way to the Loch's shore and all eyes watched as Patch swam out almost towards the middle of the loch. Suddenly the dog disappeared.

'See that, Dave?' asked Rory.

'Yup she's dived,' responded pilot David Kerr as he launched the inflatable boat into the loch.

'That a good sign?' asked Tony.

'She's found human remains. Still not confirmed its Callum, but with the clothing and the dog, it's looking very much like it. Poor mother, I feel for her.'

The inflated boat set off with both pilot and Rory aboard. Rory held a long pole with a hook at the end. The engine eventually died and Patch, the cadaver dog, having completed its grim task, struggled on board the craft and shook, spraying the men with its wet coat. Rory prodded the water and Tony could see the water was not too deep, even at the centre. The pole was not completely immersed.

Rory gave a thumbs-up then he pulled with all his might. The pole became more visible and soon the body of a young man surfaced. It took the best part of twelve minutes before the body was aboard the boat. Then the engine engaged, and they headed back to shore.

The first thing Rory did was to throw a coloured rubber ball into the water. Patch dived after it and brought it back to him. This time Rory threw it as far as he could, over the ground, and Patch set off once more.

It was pay-back time for the dog. Job completed satisfactorily but another throw was required.

'So Tony, what Sioux trick found Callum's body?' he said looking at him in anticipation.

'Well, if you must know. Instinct. With your information that it was not a murder and you had almost run out of reasonable enquiries. I recalled cases back home in similar situations. The common denominator is water. It fascinates and tempts. Loch Urie was the nearest and deepest area of fresh water from his home, albeit some distance away. But swim alone in cold open water and there's always a degree of danger. Add the deceptive autumn temperatures and the weeds at the bottom of the loch and you have the perfect storm, as it were. That's my instinct, Sioux instinct if you will, in this sad case.'

Dr. Carter confirmed Callum Dalrymple died of drowning at the University Hospital at Ayr. A fatal enquiry, conducted by the Procurator Fiscal Fiona France, was held in Ayr Sheriff Court in due course where it was established beyond reasonable doubt that Callum's death was due to misadventure, by drowning.

Word had got out in Blackwaterfoot about Callum's discovery and Tony's miraculous insight into his whereabouts, but more revelations were about to surface.

Tony was heading for his room when Robbie caught his attention.

'A word with you Tony,' stopped him in his tracks and he returned to the reception desk. Robbie was smiling.

'I've got a few Premium Bonds, not many. They occasionally send a dividend, usually £25. I never get anything more. But in today's post, just as you predicted, it was a £500 cheque. I can't thank you enough.'

Tony smiled at him and patted his shoulder. 'Don't thank me. It's the Sioux spirit within me.'

The next day, Tony received a call in his room. He lifted the phone gingerly.

'There's a Mrs. Moira Galbraith in to see you. Will you be down soon?' asked Robbie.

'Sound intriguing. I'm comin' boss.'

Tony set eyes on an ill-clad, blue rinse-haired woman on or around fifty years of age.

'Howdy Ma'am, you wish to see me?'

'Yes, I do. Well, I know the good you do around here; I was wondering, well, not sure how I can put it to you.'

'Take your time; I got most of the day.'

'Well, I'm married but you know, not really. I don't let my husband near me.'

'I guess depression. Am I on the right track?' suggested Tony.

She let out a grunt. 'Yes, I'm depressed. I know I could go to the doctor, but it's the stigma of depression. Ye ken, too many loose tongues in a small community. That's why I...'

'There's no stigma with depression. It's an illness just like a bad cold that does not go away. So, you think a Sioux potion can cure you?'

'I'm willing to give it a go.'

Tony stroked his imaginary beard. 'Can you come back here tomorrow morning?'

'I suppose so. Can you cure me?'

'No, I can never guarantee a cure, but I can make your life a whole lot better.'

For the rest of that day, Tony walked around the outskirts of the hamlet of Shiskine. His eyes were fixed on the ground before him. He was looking for a universal plant found all over America and much of Britain. It was almost 5 pm when he found what he wanted. He pulled up six thick stems of St John's Wort plant, placed them in his bag and returned to the hotel.

The following day when Mrs Moira Galbraith arrived, she was taken upstairs to Tony's room. She knocked.

Tony opened the door and invited her in. She saw the yellow weeds in a China bowl but said nothing.

'I will give you the Sioux treatment if you wish. It will not hurt but the first step is unusual. Can I ask you to run on the spot?'

'You mean here?'

'Yes, until you feel you are starting to sweat.'

Moira began with very small steps and Tony was quick to notice them. 'Try and lift your knees up as you run. You'll reach the sweating point sooner,' smiled Tony.

Meanwhile he tended the leaves, sorting them out by size.

'I see some sweat on your brow now. That's good, just a few more steps and you can relax.'

A minute later when she stopped running, she gasped. 'That's me finished. I feel I have run a marathon.' They laughed.

'Now, can I ask you to remove your jersey?'

Moira hesitated. She wondered what instruction might follow. She blurted out, 'Just my pullover?'

'Yes, that's all, I promise,' Tony laughed quietly at her reservations.

She pulled it over her head and put it on the nearby chair. Tony brought over the plant and folded it. He placed it under her sweaty arms.

'How does that feel?'

'A bit uncomfortable, I'm afraid,' she said with doleful eyes.

'Yes, it will be but it's important it stays there as long as you can hold it. You see the medicine in the St John's Wort plant is being released into your sweaty armpit. That is the closest we can get to the artery nearest your heart. The sweat is a conductor. Now it won't work immediately but I am giving you these extra leaves so you can use more at home, after you have worked up a sweat, of course.'

'And that is all?'

'It's all that the Sioux do.'

'And, er...how much do I pay you for this treatment?'

'Let me know how you feel in a couple of days. There are no costs involved at all. Nature heals. Not me.'

Chapter 6: Explosion

The Archaeology department and the Geography department of Glasgow University brought six students and two professors to Arran. Their activities were to explore the Nazi aircraft, consider if it could be saved for a museum, seek the bones and personal items for a burial, detect any historical items within the plane and finally search for any gold in the streams nearby.

Professor Sue Pierpoint was head of the Archaeology department and she set her three students off with trowels and spades to uncover more of the aircraft. Meanwhile Professor Ricky Matheson, of the Geography department set his three students on a pan search of the streams leading from Loch Tanna. They were to go 'snipping' – a process where they changed into heavy dry suits with snorkels in position. They had a better chance of detecting nuggets of gold by semi-immersing themselves in the water laterally and looking though the disturbed water with their masks and exploring hands.

After shopping at the Harbour Shop, Moira paid a visit to the hotel. Robbie informed her that Tony was sitting out on the front with a coffee. He offered Moira a coffee, but she said she'd not be stopping for long. She said so with a smile and Robbie noticed her smartly dressed winter outfit.

'I hope I am not bothering you,' she said as she nervously approached Tony. He stood up.

'Ah Moira. You sure look swell today, if I might say so. Come have a seat,' he gestured to her to sit on the bench he occupied.

Moira turned towards him. 'I'd like to thank you for seeing me the other day.'

'It was my pleasure.'

'Yes, but the St John's Wort weed has lifted my depression...er....'

'That's what I hoped it would do,' Tony interrupted.

'And if I may say, do forgive me, but we have resumed our loving relationship as well.'

'I am truly happy for you,' said a relaxed and smiling Tony.

Moira clasped her handbag on her lap. 'This Sioux treatment, I have not heard of it before. Is it easy to learn?'

'It's the Sioux way of life. Using nature to mend our ways, it's sometimes thought of as juju in my own country, but I call it insight. You want to learn it? Difficult I'd say. It took me years to learn.'

Sue arrived and joined the archaeologists at the crash site. Student Helen stopped to gauge the likely descent of the plane and concluded that it may have clipped the Beinn Tarsuinn mountain top and dived down too low to avoid the summit of Beinn Bhreac. Its final position was three quarters way between the two heights. The ground was soft there and it would not have taken too long before it had sunk into the marsh and have been buried by nature.

'It's a very remote area. The flight path would have been to fly over the northeast of Arran and proceed up the Clyde to the docks of Glasgow,' said Helen with her glasses perched on her head.

That would identify the plane as a bomber. Sue's team consisted of post graduate students Gail, Helen. and Ian. The word 'bomber' put the students on edge.

Ian, a long black-haired giant of a man, with muscles to vie with Popeye, set to freeing as much of the plane's muddy wing as he could, using a heavy-duty grubbing hoe. Gail sat beside him, a frail looking determined lass, her brush poised to clear the earth between each of Ian's strikes. They worked like ants knowing what each other was doing.

The plane's camouflaged green patches appeared in places but in other parts the paint had dissolved over time leaving the fuselage in an earthy dark grey metal. After an hour, much of the wing had appeared. Helen and her Professor marked out what should be the perimeter of the plane in white tape. It fluttered in the breeze making it difficult to be anchored at first.

Ian began attacking the clods of earth under the wing and suddenly stopped as if confronted by an unidentified animal or foe. He stood up very slowly. He looked for his professor then shouted.

'Sue, I've found the bomb casing. There seems to be a bomb inside.'

'Step back. I'm coming,' was her instant response.

Sue had not thought such an old wreck could have such a final bite, but she was sure she must not leave her students at risk.

'Get away from it, now,' she shouted, and the Archaeology department retreated some fifty yards. Sue took out her mobile phone.

'Hi Sally,' she said to her secretary at the university in Glasgow. 'Look up Army Bomb Disposal. Give them our grid reference. This German aircraft we're excavating may still pack a punch.'

They erected their tents some five hundred yards away from the aircraft making a campfire as the snorkelers returned shouting excitedly as they approached the camp. The distance was soon minimal, and their hollers became clear. They had found gold.

Five unmistakable nuggets of bright gold were shown to the archaeologists. They all crowded around to see the amazing find.

'That lot would pay for our fees a few times over,' suggested Helen whose eyes were so large a gold necklace seemed also to be on her mind.

'We have a duty to report such a find. Of course, there may be more gold in these parts, but the authorities must first identify it is gold, possibly how long it had been undetected and whose property it is. There's a lot to consider when finding precious metals,' Ricky said and lowered the expectations of the students who saw the find as "finders' keepers" in attitude.

'But Ricky, the gold find is too near the aircraft. The bomb disposal guys must take precedence here,' stated Sue.

He nodded his agreement.

It was the following morning, just after a cooked breakfast which Ricky had supervised, as mugs of tea warmed their hands and throats, the sound of a helicopter was heard overhead. It descended and the

Army markings of 'Bomb Disposal unit' were seen amid excitement.

Major Mike Blatter de Fford approached in combative attire, with his crown pips on each shoulder.

'Morning ladies and gentlemen. Glad to see a source of water handy. We will do a reconnoitre first, locate bombs then bring in 'Archie.''

'A dog?' asked a surprised Gail.

'A dog would get killed. Archie is a remote-controlled device. Rough terrain here, it will tax its ability.'

Ian liked the sharp tones of the Major but worried about his safety. 'Isn't it dangerous?' he asked.

'Most dangerous job in the army, for sure. But if we minimise the risks, we'll be content. Need to ensure we don't destroy the plane, too. It will have some historical significance.'

'Yes Major, that's crucial,' Sue agreed.

'Okay let's keep a perimeter zone in place. Don't move from your encampment. That's an order,' the Major instructed with a pointed finger. The students all sat down on the uneven ground.

The Major instructed two privates to approach the plane. It took some considerable time for them to get near the plane as their attire seemed more like that of astronauts approaching their rocket. Then the men went out of sight. They crawled towards the metal beast with caution and located the first bomb. One man opened a leaver on top of the bomb and led a rubber pipe from its aperture. The men retreated and attached a larger hose in Archie's clamped hand, and it trudged unsteadily towards the plane. It stopped. The soldier had led the hose to the loch, and he seemed to turn on the water as it snaked its way to Archie. Then a jet of water filled the bomb and the men waited.

'Not long now,' said the Major.

'You mean not long now till there's an almighty explosion?' suggested Ian.

'No sir, by flooding the bomb, we disarm it. There will be no explosion unless we disturb more bombs in the metal beast.'

The men had an idea where other bombs might be located having studied the structure of this 1940 Nazi Messerschmitt BF 109.

British cities were targeted by Nazi bombers in the Battle of Britain in 1940 and this plane, a sleek high-speed bomber, must have been heading to the ship building on the River Clyde at Glasgow, the following year. Many bombs fell short of their target and the people of Dumbarton and Clydebank suffered in 1941. The bombs were spread even wider. The grandmother of Ricky, who had as a child, written an invoice for the destruction of her Bishopton garden greenhouse and addressed it to Herr Hitler. The letter was posted. There was no reply, he told his students. They laughed.

This bomber caused no casualties then but had the capacity to do so now.

It took three more hours of dedicated work by the major's men, but Archie eventually returned to its wooden crate.

The Major confirmed to the students that the plane had been made safe and it remained almost intact for posterity. The students could now return to continue to unearth the plane.

Chapter 7 : An Italian Night

Robbie Crawford had handed over his nugget of gold to the police and was informed of the process it would take, by Rory. But as he had placed the receipt in his drawer, he knew the gold was technically still in his possession.

That afternoon, Robbie was not himself. He looked down at an open book on his desk and was looking dejected. Tony recognised his demeanour.

'What's getting you down, boss?' he asked showing concern on his face.

Robbie looked up at his guest wondering if he should tell him. After all it was none of his business. He adjusted his seating in his chair behind his desk. Then he adjusted his thoughts.

'I'm consulting a trade book, to get a chef immediately for a week or so.'

'Why what's happened?' Tony asked in a concerned manner.

'Gavin has come down with a tummy bug. I can't have him near food for a week,' Robbie said shaking his head then running his hand through his hair.

'Okay, I can solve your problem.' Tony responded with a grin of delight.

'I can't see how any Sioux medicine will solve this headache,' replied Robbie.

'I can cook. Seriously I can. Brought up by a Sicilian mother, I sure learned how to cook under her.'

Robbie looked at Tony with a wrinkled row on his forehead. ‘You mean keep our standard menu alive? Or would it be Italian?’

‘We could have an Italian night, a Nu Yok and even a Mexican night while keepin’ the usual menu in place, sure.’

‘You’ve worked in a restaurant before?’ asked Robbie still with an eye on the chef replacement list.

Tony smiled as he reminisced. ‘Mama Leone’s restaurant, downtown Nu Yok. All through my university breaks. Got to know the tricks of the trade, the use of fresh vegetables and as for my Tiramisu it’s the best in the city. You say, just a week. Perfect. Try me and see.’

‘Okay, I believe you. Can you start tomorrow?’

‘I can start this evening if you wish.

‘That doesn’t leave much time.’

‘Sure, suits me,’ said Tony rolling up his sleeves as he set off to the kitchen.

The Procurator Fiscal and Crown Office received six nuggets of gold. All the staff crowded around the rocks. Most touched the nuggets. Fiona France, Senior Prosecutor made her way into the gathering.

‘Okay, all seen enough gold?’ she asked.

‘Wish it was on my finger,’ said Gwen the middle-aged Fiscal with a greying bun at the back of her head and an impish grin.

Fiona disregarded her remark. ‘The gold is heading from here to the metallurgy department of Edinburgh University. Group 4 will escort the gold. I’m just about to sign it out.’

'But gold is gold. What will the university find that's different?' asked Gwen.

'They will be able to tell first if it is actually gold, how old it is, what strength of carat and how long it has been in the ground on Arran, too. They will also establish on whose ground the gold was found. At least that's as much as I can say.'

From the door entrance arrived three uniformed Security men who placed the gold in a cushioned metal box and then in a bag which one officer locked on to his wrist. He gave the key to one of his colleagues. They departed the Crown Office and returned to their secure transport whose engine was already running.

Tony was delighted to be in the kitchen where the cook Maggie was holding the fort. She lacked confidence in her role as cook in the circumstances, but Tony praised everything she did and encouraged her to experiment with local ingredients.

'More turmeric and parsley, in that sauce Maggie,' he suggested to her as she stirred the tomato, onions and garlic together in a sauce.

Meanwhile Tony was liquidising the soup from a pan full of oyster mushrooms, a large sweet potato, onions, garlic and three carrots. The salt-free veggie cube soon disintegrated as it mixed with the assorted vegetables and a squirt of tomato purée was the last ingredient to be added to the bubbling pot.

Robbie sat doing the hotel's accounts in his office, but his taste buds were on alert. He was distracted. He put his pen down and entered the kitchen. He liked what he smelt.

'Tony, you seem to have settled well here in Blackwaterfoot. Why not emigrate from the States and live here permanently?'

'You mean immigrate to Scotland?' Tony shouted above the din in the kitchen.

'It would be to the UK not Scotland at present, but you'd be very welcome here.'

Tony opened two more buttons on his shirt and widened the open window.

'That's what Gavin used to do about now, with all pots on the cookers,' said Maggie.

'Gavin, he's making progress with the runs?' asked Tony.

'Yes, but he won't be back till next week.'

Tony grunted. 'I only intended to come for three months on my visa. See where my ancestors came from and get to know the locals. I've almost done all of that, now.'

Maggie tapped her wooden spoon on a pan then laid it on a plate.

'You've been good for us. Finding gold, finding the Nazi plane and the missing lad, as well. You've got the knack of being there at the right time. That's for sure.'

Tony did not reply but turned to Maggie and smiled.

After the first day's meals, Robbie was delighted. Then Tony suggested Saturday night, should be Italian Night.

'If Gavin our chef could only see what's happening in his kitchen,' was his instant response. 'Then Italian it is.

Mind you it will be your second last meal. Gavin returns on Monday.'

'Then you must be relieved. But I've enjoyed being your chef,' said Tony with a smile as large as the Brooklyn Bridge.

An Italian Saturday Night advertisement went out on a billboard standing outside the hotel and by word of mouth too. Soon it had to be withdrawn. All tables had been booked. Tony planned his special meal in his bedroom at night recalling his student days at Mama Leone's restaurant in Manhattan. This was no working holiday for him, cooking was in his Italian blood. He was very much at home in the kitchen, creating mouth-watering meals. Then the menu was laminated and circulated around the lounge:

Antipasti

Ginestrata – A lightly spiced egg-based soup with chicken sauce and Masala wine.

Bruschetta al basilico di pomodoro con pioviggine balsamica - Tomato Basil Bruschetta with Balsamic Drizzle

Frutti di Mare

Guance di merluzzo su un letto di vermicelli con salsa bianca colorata di curcuma e prezzemolo. - Cod cheeks on a bed of vermicelli pasta with a white sauce coloured by turmeric and finished with sprigs of parsley.

Corso di Carne

Ragù di funghi selvatici-salsiccia con vino rosso locale. Ragù with wild mushrooms in a local red wine. (V)

Cacciatore di pollo – The hunter's chicken in a rich vegetable dish with vinegar and beans.

Una semplice pizza vegetariana con insalata e una fetta di pane all'aglio. – a simple vegetarian pizza with salad and a slice of garlic bread. (V)

Corse di Dolce

Cassata Siciliana – a round sponge cake moistened with liqueur and layered with ricotta cheese and candied fruit.

Tiramisù al miele – Honey tiramisu. Il miele filtrava in una pasta filo imbevuta di vino Marcela. Servito con gelato locale di qualsiasi gusto o crema pasticcera. Honey seeped in a filo pastry soaked in Marcela wine. Served with local ice cream of any flavour or custard.

The local Blackwaterfoot residents had watering mouths for days after seeing this Italian meal advertised. And all for £12 as the meal was to be subsidised by Tony. But complaints arose. “More than the restaurant could possibly take,” was all Robbie could say until Tony suggested that the Italian night could become ‘nights’ if he was allowed to resume in the kitchen for a final Sunday Italian meal. Once more Robbie found Tony’s suggestion for an additional night, sensible and most welcome.

At the tables, people discussed the impact Tony was having on their community. Unsurprisingly a few felt he was a typical loud New Yorker with all the answers at his fingertips, bombastic and forthright, they claimed. Not as reserved as the locals were.

‘That’s hardly fair,’ said Morag, a widow who could not resist an Italian meal. ‘I mean we could have found the gold or the aircraft ourselves if we hadn’t sat by our fires most of the winter and got out into the wilds of the island.’

‘Aye but wasn’t it canny that he found Callum’s body so easily. I mean surely the police had tipped him off to enhance his credibility in the island?’ suggested resident imbiber Eric.

Morag gasped. ‘That’s a bit far-fetched, Eric. You say there are corrupt police officers here on Arran? I doubt that very much. Rory Murdoch is a gem of a man. Be what it may, Tony’s a fine Italian cook. You can’t pass that by,’ she said in a manner to end the conversation agreeably.

No sooner had Morag spoken when the strains of an accordion was heard. Tony appeared having sung the introduction of *O Sole Mio* out of sight. He had a fine tenor voice, and his unexpected entertainment went down a treat. The diners' eyes seemed transported to somewhere in rural rustic Italy at that moment.

Then Tony smiled at the applause which came his way. He acknowledged their approval with a nod, so he continued with a more poignant song in *Senza una Donna* (Without A Woman.) Levant's *Tikibombom* was a little avant-garde for the Blackwaterfoot assembled diners, but they listen respectfully as Tony's fingers ran up and down the vertical keyboard on his right hand while his left hand magically found the right buttons to press as the living instrument's lungs moved in a lateral sweep.

'My, Tony's multi-thingamybobed, isn't he?' asked Moira with a pleasing smile stretched over her face.

'Aye, he's certainly multitalented.'

'Ah that's the word I was searching for,' Moira replied, slapping Robbie's back in fun.

'At least he's put that accordion to good use. It has not been played since Wullie Barr died some two years ago.'

'Yes, Wullie was a good accordionist. As you say, Tony's given it a good airing. This Tony has some remarkable gifts, hasn't he?' suggested Moira.

'He certainly has,' replied Robbie showing a proud air as if Tony was perhaps a relation.

Chapter 8: A Manhattan Breakfast Bar

Word was out. Hugh Boag of the Arran Banner wrote a splendid article about Tony, his links to Blackwaterfoot and his activities in finding Callum's body, the Nazi aircraft, and the gold as well as his successful predictions.

The Glasgow Herald and the Scotsman, The Times and the Observer as well as a myriad of tabloids had alerted the public to the gold and the Nazi plane discovered in northern Arran.

Arran was accessible as it was not far from Glasgow. But arriving on Arran was by boat and in fair weather. It put off hordes of gold prospectors, but some 69 gold diggers arrived with pans intent on making their fortune while historians made for the ever-surfacing plane before it could be dispatched to the mainland.

Tony was invited to see the removal of the plane and give an interview to the BBC. He attended at the aircraft sight having passed the hordes of gold diggers. It made him feel guilty. He knew there was no gold left in the streams but the enthusiasm in which the gold seekers had approached their work was heartening. It may have been a welcomed diversion from their ordered lives, thought Tony. That thought appeased his guilt.

'You say you had special powers to locate this plane?' asked John Dignan of the Daily Record.

Tony looked puzzled. 'The aircraft,' he said, 'I just came across it. I detected the disfiguration of the land. It was not normal. I investigated and hey presto the plane appeared after I had scraped along what turned out to be a wing.'

'So, no Sioux insight here?' asked the journalist with a smirk of a smile.

'No, the weather had slowly revealed this piece of history. Rather like the sandstorms on Orkney that laid bare Skara Brae,' Tony replied recalling his British history of his school days.

'I see. And what about finding gold on Arran?' ventured the journalist.

'That's more of a Sioux insight. I was led to that stream. Why? I don't know but yes, I found a nugget of gold,' said Tony while looking away.

'There have been a total of six nuggets so far, in fact. Do you suspect there are more gold nuggets in the hills?' asked John.

'There's been gold found nearby on Argyll over the past decade. The land in the north of Arran is similar to Kintyre, you know?'

John wrote at speed and as he did so, a man approached.

'Excuse me, Mr Lupino?'

Tony turned towards the man dressed in a smart dark suit. He had a miniscule lapel badge which bore three colours on it. Perhaps, Belgium or Germany, thought Tony as he replied.

'Yes, I'm Tony.'

'I am pleased to meet you. My name is Jurg Maurer, German Ambassador to the United Kingdom,' he said as he proffered out his hand.

Tony shook it firmly, in a business fashion. 'I see. So you are up from London, I guess.'

'Indeed. I was informed that some bones and uniform have been uncovered. Sufficient for my Government to seek the return of the bones for a private or military funeral.'

'I see,' said Tony wondering if a military funeral was possible given the passing of time.

'Of course, I understand. But a military funeral?'

Herr Maurer paused. He looked at Tony. 'There are grandchildren of the deceased. They want a formal military farewell. Er...you are of Italian background not so?'

'Well yes, but fourth generation, American too.'

Jurg Maurer nodded. 'A military air crash, body remains detected; it should be a military funeral.'

'I see. There must be sensitivities around. It was an enemy air crash, in a world war where many died and were not individually honoured, on both sides. Of course, the remains will be carefully gathered and returned to Germany, I am sure. A funeral is of course expected but a military funeral might cause resentment in Britain.'

'You are right, but these were just not airmen doing their duty as they saw fit at the time. We have the flight identified with its number and there are family members in Germany who remember who they were. They are few but they are also leading the call for a military funeral. That is why I wanted to visit this site.'

'Okay, I get it. It's not my decision of course but their descendants can sure have closure now.'

Jurg nodded and offered his hand. 'Without you finding this aircraft, we would not have met. It has been my pleasure meeting you, Mr Lupino.'

Tony shook the Ambassador's hand. 'We are no longer enemies. May their remains be honoured, and the family's needs be met.'

'Excuse me, United Photographers. Can I have a shot of you both?'

Snaps went off like a volley of bullets. It must have been around fifty shots were taken in total, over a very short moment of time.

'I have a contract with many periodicals and papers. It makes sure you are not over photographed,' the snapper said.

'That's a relief,' said Tony.

'I could not agree more,' said Jurg Maurer.

A week later, Danny Berlotti sauntered along the sidewalk to his breakfast bar in Manhattan. There he enjoyed his usual Saturday feast of a tower of pancakes, smothered in Vermont syrup. His mind was relaxed as he munched through the dough and washed it down with both a black coffee and a zero sugar Coke. Sitting diagonally opposite him, was a man engrossed in his newspaper with a plate of two sunny side-up eggs, sausage, tomato and bacon. He was almost bent over his newspaper. Danny strained to see the headline and gave up. Instead, he ordered a fresh orange and a doughnut to go. He paid and with his hands full he walked out of the diner passing the man. This time he saw the newspaper banner and the headline stared back at him.

He stopped at the first news seller on the next corner and bought the New York Times and set off home. As soon as he was in his palatial penthouse suite, he boiled the kettle. The mug of strong Italian coffee was in his hands when he sat down and dialled his cousin.

'Hey, Arne? Danny here.'

'Hi.'

'I've located the devil.'

'You mean you know where Tony is?'

'Yes. He's at Arran.'

'Iran? God why is he there? Has he become a Muslim?' asked Arne in a strangled high voice.

Danny laughed raucously. 'No, not Iran, accent is on the A ... Arran, an island in Scotland.'

'Okay. So, the Nu Yok attorneys gave him leave? And he comes to Scotland. Strange?'

'I dunno, but he's sure on his own now. That much is true and looks like he'll be there a while. It gives us a golden opportunity.'

'For a while, yea? How do you know that?'

'It's in the Nu Yok Times today. He's found some goddamn gold and some Nazi plane. He's become a bit of a celebrity.'

'Good grief. What d'ya mean a Nazi plane?'

'Just what it says in the paper let me see...here it is...New York lawyer, Tony Lupino sets heather alight with findings of gold and a World War Two German bomber on the Scottish island of Arran.'

'Wow. I got ya. So, he's inherited the gold legally, it seems. So, will you or I get a British visa?'

'I think we should meet and plan what we can do. It might be our only opportunity, for a long time. The devil must have sent me my citation I got on the day he departed the US,' said Danny.

'Hey, when's you due in court?'

'January 17th,' said Danny. 'But I'll nut be goin' and Tony won't be dair either.'

'Yeah, I know exactly what ya mean,' said Arne with a broad smile, in his crisp Nu Yok accent.

Hugh Boag's newspaper article had found a 'stringer' in New York. He filed a copy of the piece in the city. And so, The New York Times printed Tony's activities. That news had reached Tony in a New York Google the previous evening.

Chapter 9: The Mafia's Revenge

Tony strolled along Blackwaterfoot beach kicking the seaweed which lay dejected before his path. The sun peaked through some fluffy white clouds as he progressed. But his thinking had momentarily stalled. The wind was minimal but enough to trouble calm seas and that was the only voice he heard, save for the occasional clicking sound of golfers as they hit their balls on the nearby Shiskine golf course.

What he could not get out of his mind was who in New York had possibly read the article, and knew he was on Arran? The distance was irrelevant. He looked at his watch. It told him it was 27th November. He'd be home in less than one month.

In New York, Danny Berlotti was fine-tuning his plan. He was tipped off about a certain drug. He discovered that the poisonous substance Carbofuran exhibits toxicity, mediated by the same mechanism as that of the notorious V-series nerve agents and presents a fatal risk to human life. It is classified as an extremely hazardous substance and is now banned in most countries. His research, however informed him it was easily acquired in the markets of downtown Nairobi, Kenya, where hunters purchased it to kill lions. He smiled. He had a contact there and he phoned him.

'Hi Pete. Danny here.'

'Oh Danny, cuz, yeah, good to hear ya. You visitin' Kenya?'

'I hope so and soon. Bottom line, can you get me some good quality Carbofuran?'

'Sure can. You know what it's for?'

'For my purposes, it's gotta be effective. Got ma meaning?'

'Yeah sure, for Tony, right?'

Danny gave a wicked smile and nodded as he alerted Pete of his plan.

'Some raptors are killed with it. They give it to rats, or even cats and dogs which kill them instantly and the birds of prey appear. It's effective to kill lions and other dangerous wildlife too. Some are prize species.'

'So why kill the raptors?' asked townie Danny.

'They give them to taxidermists who stuff them and then they sell them. There's a big market for them worldwide. Especially Eastern Europeans buy them up. Good prices. Er....so, how much do you need? Presumably enough to kill just one man?'

'Yeah, you got it in one. Tony Lupino. He's gone too far.'

'Yeah, he has, hasn't he? Okay can you give me 24 hours to get the stuff?'

'Just swell, I'll need that time to get two visas.'

'Two visas?'

'Yes, one to Kenya and one to Scotland.'

'I think you mean the UK. I don't think Scotland is independent yet.'

'Yea, well I get confused is it GB, UK or England?'

'Head for the British Embassy on-line.'

'Of course, cuz, thanks.'

'So, Danny, see you soon, eh?'

'Yeah, it's been too long. Some three years, I reckon.'

'Mind you bring me some Vermont syrup,' he instructed with crossed fingers.

Danny laughed. 'None but the best. I'll order a pot right away. Take care. Bye.'

Tony returned to the hotel and saw Robbie in the bar, serving customers. He went to the counter and ordered an Arran Blond.

Robbie winked at him 'Not too many blonds on Arran, will a brunette do?' he asked with a grin on his face.

'I'm a thirsty man, reflecting on the humour of the Brits. I'll have my blond in a glass if I may?'

Tony watched the froth as it diminished and the golden liquid settle.

'You've got Chutes and Ladders in the lounge, I see.'

'Sorry,' said Robbie looking at a loss.

'You call them snakes and ladders. Okay ladders go up, we agree, but snakes? Do they really go down? Chutes, I tell you.'

'I've never thought about that,' he replied.

'On your menu, you have a starter. You need a gun for a starter down our way, but hey you know, we call the starter the appetizer,' Tony laughed. 'But when I worked in the kitchen, I had my instructions cut down to size. Grill you say, broil we say. And when you shower on some hundreds and thousands (of what I might ask) we call them just sprinkles. So, you see same language different words.'

'You are an education on legs Tony. You could be a schoolteacher,' suggested Robbie.

'Me a teacher? No way. I could get through one day, but a week let alone a term, no way. No, the law is specific, suits me.'

'Do you have a specialist area in the law? I mean, is it just taking on what cases the police bring to you, or do you specialise?'

Tony took a long sip of his beer. He turned to Robbie and began to nod his head.

'I've not really talked about my work as a prosecutor. I've done some high-profile cases. I'm talking about breaking up the Italian Mafia in Nu Yok. You don't hear so much about them these days.'

Robbie looked at the ceiling thinking through Tony's response and imagining his caseload. Something crossed his mind. He just had to ask.

'But your name Tony Lupino, that's an Italian name, surely. I guess you have some sort of an advantage taking on these cases.'

'You got it in one.'

'I mean there could be some backlash from those sort of cases,' Robbie suggested.

'As I say, you got it in one. And that's why I am having a break on Arran.'

'You could have come during summer. We usually get good weeks when it's warm and with this global warming, sometimes very hot.'

Tony nodded his agreement. 'Yea that seems to make sense but, in the summer, I got no break, it was a big case started late May, it went on to late September. Then I thought about Alban Caskie. And so, I came, here.'

'The case, got a good verdict then?

'Yup three got life with no release or parole.'

'End their days in prison. Serious stuff.'

'Murderers all of them. Some six Italian/Nu Yokers gunned down in the Bronx. Down in the southern states they would be on death row. They kill them there, by the score. Up State in Nu Yok we let them languish their days thinking of their crimes. Not sure which way I would go if I had been them.'

'Me neither,' said Robbie drying a pint glass in an absent-minded manner.

As he held the cool glass in his hand Tony received a pat on the back by Eric, the resident drinker.

'So, going to apply for British citizenship? You'd certainly bring a sparkle to Blackwaterfoot,' he said as he clinked his glass against Tony's.

'Vive la difference. I like your slower way of life. It's made me reassess mine. Good for the heart rate. But the dollars come from my work and by the time I'm ready to retire, I'll possibly be too old to adapt here.'

Eric nodded as he looked into his glass. 'I don't think I could settle in New York either.'

'More's the pity,' came a remark from the snug. It was hard to identify the voice and Eric's vision was impaired with the amount he had drunk. His repose was to laugh. 'I'll have another Robbie,' he asked.

'I suggest you have had one too many, Eric.'

Eric looked lost, then he came to. 'I've just had three drinks you know, Robbie.'

'Aye three drinks after lunch and two in the morning. Mixing your whisky with your dark ale. I'm doing you a favour Eric. Enough is enough.'

Eric turned and staggered out of the bar muttering something about America and its drink laws being better there.

'You've got some bottle Robbie. Try that downtown Nu Yok and the guns come out. At least you'd be taken round the back of the bar and given a good hiding.'

'I can't say that does not happen in Glasgow, but here on Arran, we sort of care for each other. Antiquated you might think, but it's the way we are.'

Chapter 10: Nairobi Provides

Danny arrived in the sweltering heat, of the oven baked air of Jomo Kenyatta Airport, Kenya. He entered the air-conditioned airport terminal, cleared customs, and struggled through the crowd of smiling faces to find a white hand go up at the back of the assembled families. Danny made his way through to the white man but as he approached him their eyes met. This was not Pete.

'Hey Danny, over here,' a voice shouted on Danny's left.

Out of breath came Pete weaving his way through a myriad of African families dressed in colourful clothes. He grabbed Tony in a bear hug.

'Good to see you again. Hey, you are lookin' swell.'

'You too, Pete,' said Danny releasing himself from his cousin's grip.

'Okay follow me, the car's over this way,' he pointed with his head, fearing an arm might confront someone.

They left the air conditioned cool airport to cross the short-stay park and reached his car. Its roof was down.

'No risk in leaving the hood down?'

'Nothing inside to take.'

'Except the car, perhaps?'

Pete showed him a fob. 'They need this disabling fob to get it going.'

They exited and set off down the wide Airport North route. Pete slowed down. 'I need to get some Naira from the bank here.'

He drove into the car park and got out.

'Should I come with you?'

'No Danny, admire the city. You won't be staying long.'

Pete returned from the Bank of Africa, and they proceeded further into town. They parked on a side street and walked a short distance into Maasai market.

'You got the drug?'

'No Danny. We're goin' na pick some up this morning. I ain't had time.'

'Okay. I'm with ya,' said Danny taking a deep breath. Go with the flow, he heard himself think. As long as they kept together in this rugby maul of a busy market.

Danny was overcome with the smell of rotting tomatoes and bananas. But his senses were sharpened by the colour of the produce and the market women selling their wares. Materials of different patterns were hung up like washing to dry and every vegetable and fruit seemed to be in great supply. They proceeded past some tailor kiosks with singer sewing machines hard at work repairing clothes. The market was exceptionally busy, but Danny kept a constant eye on Pete who walked slightly ahead of him. Then Pete stopped and pointed up an opening alley. Danny followed. After a couple of dozen steps forward, Pete stopped at a watch seller's stall. Rows of watch straps were lined up regimentally at the front while the faces of the straps smiled with their hands all set at ten minutes to two. Pete greeted the owner like a long-lost friend.

'Paul, this is my brother Danny from New York.'

Paul supported his right hand at his right elbow. Danny shook it.

'You are very welcome in Nairobi, Mr Danny.'

‘Thank you. It’s quite an experience. The colour is what has struck me. It’s so up front.’

‘Yes, we love colour.’

Danny’s eyes returned to the trays of watches. ‘I see it’s ten to two here. Some two hours later than my watch,’ he queried with a quizzical smile.

‘Your watch is right. It is ten to twelve.’

‘So why are all the watches set at ten to two?’ Danny asked once more.

‘If I set them all at twenty to four, I’d not sell many. The watches would look sad. So, I run them down and put smiles of the faces at Ten to Two,’ he laughed at the simplicity of the arrangement which seemed to interest the American.

‘Okay, Paul. Have you got it?

‘Yes, come inside.’

Inside was through a draped cloth where three different seats surrounded the area and the cash register sat on an old shoogly wooden table.

Paul opened the drawer beneath the cash register and brought out a bag. It was a tartan bag. The weave was green and blue with a red line horizontal and vertical in squares over it. He opened it. Inside the lining was another bag of clear plastic in which the powder lay.

‘Morrison tartan, should you be asked,’ said Pete.

‘It’s more than you will need; it’s sufficient. Too much and it slips on to your skin and I’ll be going to your own funeral, get my drift?’

‘Yeah, but what I don’t understand is if it is legal to sell in Kenya, why the secrecy? Why’s the deal done behind a curtain?’

'It be sort of legal to sell, but you need a license to sell it. I don't pay the licence so that's why we hide it from the authorities.'

'I see,' said Danny being very much at the beck and call of his Kenyan operatives.

'Sure, don't want to die with this stuff,' said Danny as Pete unwound a bundle of Naira notes and handed them over to Paul. He counted them as if a bank clerk flicking the notes with the fingers of one hand and mouthing the total.

'Good to do business with you, Paul.'

'You are very kind to me Masta. Thank you.'

'I'll see you next week about a cocaine supply. How is that going Paul?'

'Yes, I'll have it for you, most certainly.'

'Till then,' said Pete.

Danny shook his hand as he said goodbye.

They walked through the sweet-smelling market amid pleas to buy jewellery for their wives, bananas for the children and tobacco for granddad. But Danny had none of these relatives and told them so. It did not put the traders off.

'Then some chocolate pebbles, here a bag for you,' an elderly market woman gestured.

Danny's heart was compromised. 'Hey Pete, you got some change for the chocolate?'

Pete returned with his hand fiddling in his pocket.

He offered 75 Kenyan shillings.

'Oh Masta, not enough to feed my children.'

He opened his hand and gave her one hundred and fifty Kenyan shillings. 'That's all I have.'

'Okay,' she said handing the bag of chocolate pebbles to Danny.

As they walked away and Danny began to open his chocolate pebbles, he asked. '150 shillings? That not a bit steep?'

'One dollar is 37 cents. You think your chocolates are not worth that?'

'Just as well I fly tomorrow. I'll never get the hang of the Kenyan shilling,' said Danny shaking his head. He offered a chocolate to Pete.

He looked into the paper poke and selected a red coated chocolate. Danny had a green one.

Back at Pete's palatial white walled detached home, he summonsed his cook steward, Andrew, to bring two glasses of cold passion fruit juice. Then he lowered his voice. 'Beer later, we need to discuss the Carbofuran with clear heads.'

Danny nodded.

They made their way through to the garden at the back of the house. Crickets seemed to accompany them in their clicking symphony and attractive butterflies fluttered around the Frangipani and the Bougainvillea bushes. A cat slithered past the seat in which Danny sat, before it leapt up and curled on his lap.

'That's Buckley. He'll soon settle. He's a rag-doll cat. They love human contact. He does not leave the compound, stays in the house all day.'

'Yeah, they are popular in Nu Yok apartments, back home.'

'Okay, first how ya gonna get the drug past UK customs?'

'You had any experience?'

'Yeah, placed a bag of stolen sterling notes in each sock. Got through no problem. Mind you they might look at your shoes.'

'Surely, I can do it with the bag in one of my socks then?'

Pete shook his head. 'With your weight on the bag, it could busts and you'd be dead in a few minutes, with this stuff.'

Pete pulled out two pens. Neither had ink in them. Danny inspected them.

'Look normal pens to me.'

'Open one.'

Danny did. As he unscrewed it, he found no ink but the ball point remained at the end.

'The pens you can fill when you are ready to kill him. Use these rubber gloves,' he said as he handed them over. 'Either find his car then leave a trace of the powder on the back of his driving wheel if you get access to it or the external door handle if you don't. If you get into his room, leave a trace on any lace-up shoe. Get the stuff on the inside tongue of his shoe and it will seep into his foot. Dead in ten minutes. It depends on what you find in Blackwaterfoot, but the bag will give you enough to refill. You'll find a way, I'm sure of that. I don't have to tell you that the stakes are so high.'

The cold drinks arrived. Andrew set the drinks down on a glass table situated between the two schemers. He laid down a plate of fried plantain and some cashew nuts.

'If you wish anything else, call me. I am always at your service, Mastas.'

'Thank you, Andrew. I sure am ready for this cold drink,' said Danny, taking a handful of fried plantain as he spoke.

As soon as Andrew was out of earshot, Pete returned to the plot.

'You studied Arran?'

'Well, it seems Tony is at Blackwaterfoot. There's only one substantial hotel there, the Kinloch.'

'Yeah, but you can't stay there. He'd soon pick up the vibes and leave. You gotta find a B&B.'

'A what?'

'A Bed and Breakfast place. Usually, the host lives in the same house so a ruse has to be devised. Thought about that?'

'Well, it's a holiday island so I'll say I'm on holiday.'

Pete shook his head. 'It's almost December Danny. People don't go on holiday to Arran in December.'

Danny realised there was much more planning required. Then he had a thought.

'I could be an ornithologist. Come to see the winter birds on Arran. So, what about that?'

'Yeah, sounds good, but...'

'I was expecting a 'but'...so what's the problem?'

'We'd better find you the right clothing, binoculars, notepad. You gotta look the part.'

Danny smiled as he thought through this new role. 'Then I guess it's back to the market.'

Pete shook his head and called out Andrew. Andrew came out walking smartly to the table.

'Andrew, can you buy some binoculars. I mean second hand. Used ones, if possible, a notebook and pen and a tweed cap if you can.'

'A tweed hat, sir. It would be very warm to wear a tweed hat here.'

'I know but Danny flies to Scotland tomorrow and it's cold there in winter. Bloody cold all year, I hear too.'

'I know that sir. I had a Scottish masta many years ago; he gave me the name Andrew, like the Patron Saint of Scotland. I love the bagpipes the Kenyan Police play and the Scottish country dancing. I love Scotland.'

'Do you know where Arran is, Andrew?' asked a surprised Danny.

'Arran, masta? I think it is an island. I'm not sure if it is inhabited. Maybe it is.'

That night Danny lay out his disguise. He felt the deerstalker hat was perhaps a size slightly too small, but the tight fit was quite comfortable. Pete had provided a knapsack into which he placed his notepad and his pen. He rehearsed his lines as an ornithologist and Pete had given him a book about European birds. His plan was to arrive on Arran, find accommodation, keep a low profile, get to know Tony's movements then go in for the kill and beat a hasty retreat to Nu Yok. There he could have a party. Job done.

Jomo Kenyatta International Airport seemed very familiar having been there only two days ago, but this would be his first hurdle. Pete had devised his plan to hide some of the drug by purchasing a bird book which he altered by cutting a square in the book to contain the plastic bag of powder. The book lay in his shoulder bag along with two other bird books and his binoculars. His drug loaded pens were attached to his jacket.

At customs he took out the books and binoculars and placed the books on top of each other beside the bag. He saw his collection of ornithological paraphernalia slowly proceed along a conveyor belt into an x-ray box. Danny's heart was in his mouth as he stood, arms wide open coming out of the body scan archway. He looked towards the books and found no-one having any interest in them. He put his slippered shoes on as casually as he could and reassembled his shoulder bag with its contents. As he was about to leave the conveyor belt, he saw two custom officers stir their mugs of tea. He smiled at them, and they caught his eye. They smiled back at Danny, and one wished him a safe journey.

The flight took just over four hours and was largely uneventful except an inquisitive and forward young lady asked why he was flying to Glasgow from Italy. Perhaps he was a football scout as Glasgow Rangers were due to play Roma next month. She put that theory to Danny.

'Soccer? No, not my game. I'm having an ornithological trip to Scotland. That's all.'

'Where will you visit?' she enquired leaning over the vacant seat between each other.

'I'm thinking of spending some time on Arran,' he said hoping that might end her enquiries.

'I hope you see a golden eagle,' she said with an engaging smile.

'I hope so too,' he replied and took out one of his bird books to read.

Robbie approached Tony as he gazed out to sea, towards Carradale, with a cappuccino in his hands.

‘Tony, I hope you don’t mind me asking, but you don’t seem to have a mobile phone with you. Especially you are being an American.’

Tony guffawed. ‘I’m on holiday. I never take one when I’m off duty. No point going on a break with a cell phone, is there? I have an i-pad though.’

‘I sort of agree with you about a phone but still take mine. Never know when the kids are in trouble,’ suggested Robbie.

‘Kids, trouble. Yeah, that’s why I never married.’

‘What you never married? I thought you said you were widowed?’

‘Yeah,’ thought Tony very quickly. A traditional Sioux wedding is not authorised by the State, so I guess I was not really married to her, was what I meant. We certainly lived together but had no children.’

‘I see,’ said Robbie instantly. ‘Handsome guy like you. Bet you broke a few hearts along the way,’ Robbie said.

‘Don’t mean I haven’t had a few girlfriends,’ said Tony glad to have overcome that hurdle.

Chapter 11: Miss Anderson the Hostess

The plane cut through low cloud unveiling glimpses of Glasgow. The spires of the Cathedral and the river Clyde met Danny's eyes. He was surprised at the size of the city suddenly appearing beneath its wings. He was also struck by the vivid colour of the hills to the north of the city and the green fields to the south. He had never seen this vibrant natural green colour before. He commented on this to the girl in the seat beside him.

'Rain. That's what it does. It washes the grass, the fields, and the mountains. We have lots of rivers. Yes, rain and a climate which does not set the heather alight. No extremes. Just like its folk. Practical, no-nonsense people, you'll find.'

'Suits me. Change is what a holiday is all about.'

'You said you are from New York, didn't you?'

'Yes, why?'

'There are few similarities between New York and Glasgow. Your city is a place of extremes in weather, people, food, gun laws, ...'

'Your police don't have guns?'

'No, only for big crime. You won't see police on the streets with guns.'

'We've always had a right to arm ourselves. It's what being an American is.'

'The genie is out of the bottle, that's your problem. You'll always have guns on the streets,' she concluded and added for good measure, 'kill people that's what guns do.'

Twenty minutes later, Danny collected his case from the carrousel and proceeded through the Nothing To Declare green notice. He felt unseen eyes on him.

A customs official pointed at him.

'A moment sir. Your passport please.'

Danny's hand was shaking as he pulled out his American passport. The official looked at it flicking through its pages.

'A vacation in December? Got family and friends in Scotland?'

'No, just a few days break. I'm a keen ornithologist. Hope to get some good photos of birds I've not seen before. Winter breeders like the Crossbill. They like the winter pine seed, you understand?' said Danny quoting from his bird book.

'Crossbills? I'd suggest go west young man. Try some of the islands for Sea eagles and the like. They call you a twitcher, in America, do they?

'Twitcher,' clarified Danny feeling the word instantly put him on edge.

'Yes, twitchers, bird spotters.'

'I see. We just call ourselves bird spotters.'

'You a member of a bird club in the States, then?'

'A recently formed club. Started off on a trip to Central park and we meet twice a month.'

'Then I won't keep you back, sir. Good to meet a fellow twitcher.'

'Guess I'm a twitcher now too,' suggested Danny with a relaxed laugh and as the interview came to an end, he manufactured an innocent smile.

At the Arnold Clark desk Danny booked a VW ID3 electric car.

'Where are you heading, sir?'

Danny felt ill at ease. What was that to do with her? A bland response came from his lips. 'Around Scotland.'

'If you are going north, the very north, the electricity points are less frequent.'

'Oh, I see thanks. What about Arran, I might go there?'

'Arran's well connected. Best to top up when you arrive at Brodick. But there are quite a few standpoints there, you'll find,' she said handing him the keys to the car. 'Go through this door behind me and someone will take you to your vehicle. Have a safe and enjoyable holiday, sir.'

'Thank you I will,' Danny replied feeling the Scots he had met were relaxed and interested in each other and their visitors.

Danny was pleased to have arrived so easily at Ardrossan on the Ayrshire coast but there was an ominous flag flying at the port. He learned that rough seas were pounding the harbour and it would be touch and go whether the boat would be sailing.

Danny took out his cell phone and searched for a nearby village to Blackwaterfoot. Shiskine seemed the right distance away. Shiskine B&B found Saddell View Guest House and he dialled.

'Hello, Miss Anderson speaking,' said a quiet, infirm sounding voice.

'Hi, I'm Danny from Nu Yok, a bird spotter I mean twitcher, as you say. Can I have a room for a few days?'

'Yes, you can. I don't get many bookings in December so you can stay as long as you wish. Only I go to bed early about half past nine at night. If you are out later, do keep quiet. I'm possibly reading the scriptures in bed. There's no smoking. If you do, that can be done outside. Oh, and I presume you will be having a cooked breakfast?'

'No worries about the time, I'm not a night owl either. And I don't smoke. But I'd just love a cooked breakfast.'

'Then you are most welcome. It's £35 per night but £28 if you stay for longer than three days.'

'That's just swell. A very good price. You sure you get enough to make ends meet?'

'The Good Lord provides for me, and He tells me not to make a huge profit but accept the guest with an open heart.'

'I'm really looking forward to staying with you. I'm not sure when the sailing will be. I'm at Ardrossan and they are not sure if there will be a sailing at all.'

'There will be a sailing. Have faith. I'll pray for a safe sailing for you too.'

Three quarters of an hour later it was announced over the tannoy sound system that the captain had agreed to sail but he also informed passengers that aluminium trays would be made available for all those feeling queasy.

The word queasy was not a word Danny was familiar with, but he understood what sickness was. His hair went in different directions as he returned to his car in lane two. He checked his shoulder bag. All three books were inside, and they would stay put when he was above deck.

But first he removed the bag and placed it in the foot well of the passenger's seat making it less visible. The cars inched forward until Danny's VW was on the slipway. The boat clattered as the entrance plate rattled on the quay beneath. His tyres took the force of the movement forward and clattered it down as he drove gingerly and parked eight inches behind an Audi.

Following the example of other drivers, he got out of his car, locked it and made for the metal steps to go up a floor. The kitchen was preparing meals, but the smell of food was not what Danny wanted. He climbed another floor and made his way out onto the deck, taking with him an aluminium tray on his way. A fresh wind cooled him down. He raised his collar and zipped up his jacket to his chin.

His unoccupied hand was in his pocket. He changed it with the tray hand from time to time, to keep his hands warm. The sea air mixed with the fumes of the ship as it prepared to sail and soon his container was accepting the contents of Danny's stomach.

He sat down on an empty metal barred seat as the ship shunted backwards at first, to face forward and the choppy water. Seagulls fought to regain their balance like light aircraft caught in a crosswind. The sea was churning waves of white water and a grey seal was seen enjoying the fortune of such disturbed water as it struggled to eat a tentacle lashing squid. Danny took gulps of sea air to calm his stomach. The misery was to continue for another hour but as land approached, he saw the majestic Goat Fell on the right of the island. Wild, rough land. There was bound to be eagles up that way, he thought, and so Miss Anderson would be informed that was where he would be heading.

The breaths of fresh sea air into his lungs helped to settle some nerves but he wondered how wise this mission was. He certainly had not anticipated feeling so miserable getting to Arran. Even the tail end of hurricanes from the southern Gulf of Mexico States hit New York less severely, he was convinced.

The order to return drivers to their vehicles was welcome but the progress to the car floor was anything but easy. Danny grabbed a rail as his body swung from side to side. He was sure he was being bruised as he progressed. He held onto car door handles as he made his way towards his. One door he grabbed opened. He slammed it shut hoping the car's occupants were not yet in sight. Then a woman lost her balance in front of him and would have fallen to the ground but for Danny catching her and supporting her until she regained her balance. She thanked him profusely. He grunted, feeling a kind word far from his lips as further bruising felt apparent in his ribs.

The ship drew alongside the quay and a grating thud was heard. The boat had drifted uncontrollably towards the pier and collided with it. This set off an automatic hooter and it blared until its silence brought a degree of relief and satisfaction. Progress docking resumed.

Danny was relieved when his car finally left the boat and arrived on the island. He remembered to keep to the left of the road as he entered Brodick. He saw the Co-op had an electric point, so he made for its car park noticing a warning: "For Customer's Use Only". How strict might they be, he wondered. Then, for a brief moment he worried if his Carbofuran could be found or attract police attention. Then his game would be up. He made sure his car was locked, checking it twice.

He sauntered into the large supermarket to meet the store's requirements at the e-points and lifted a basket. He selected some chocolate candy, a local newspaper, and a pack of four beers. He delayed as long as possible eyeing the store's offerings of every kind, to benefit from a good electrical top-up.

Almost a half hour later he paid by card and the goods were placed in a disposable plastic bag. He disengaged from the source of the electricity and proceeded on the String road across the island. The land was white with snow, but the road well salted and the ever-present snow poles were good guides. He admired the beauty of the high land as he changed to a lower gear.

Twenty-three minutes later he was in the outskirts of the Shiskine village. He slowed down. His eyes were pealed for the Saddell View Guest house despite Miss Anderson telling him it was on the main road. He progressed until the village was almost ending but the penultimate house set back from the road, a substantial stone building was before him. He drove into the driveway and then left into the B&B car park. He looked at his watch 7:35pm. Miss Anderson was sure to be up if not engaged in her prayers for a safe arrival for her guest. The door opened and a smiling woman with grey hair probably mid-70s Danny thought, awaited his arrival. He gathered his baggage carefully and approached her.

'Welcome to Saddell View. On a clear day you can just see the village of Saddell on the Kintyre peninsular'.

'I might see that tomorrow. Just seen Brodick, a smart wee town as you say.'

Miss Anderson scowled. Brodick is not a town, it's a village. In fact, there are no towns on the island, they are all villages.'

'Well, I never, but sure Shiskine is a quiet village,'

'That's the way God planned it. Come away in for a cup of tea. Let me boil the kettle and show you your room.'

Danny followed her upstairs to his room.

'I sleep downstairs and admit I am a little deaf. I won't hear you even if you play some music or watch the television. There's a set up there, in your room. Temperamental I am afraid; the signal is not too strong, you understand? Shiskine is a wee village, quite unlike New York. And the land rises behind the house.'

Danny smiled and gave out a quiet laugh at her remark. They entered the room and Danny put down his cases. He saw a hand basin and a toilet en suite.

'Just fine and dandy Miss Anderson. I'll sure be happy here.'

'You are not the first New Yorker to be in these parts.'

'Really?' replied Danny in apparent surprise. 'And who else has been here?'

'Oh, not in Shiskine. He's quite a celebrity. Party tricks, lectures, finding gold and a missing WW II plane, even found the body of Callum, one of our Lamlash boys who went missing. Oh, how I have prayed for his mother. She must be at her wits end.'

'I guess so. She would welcome your prayers, I am sure.' A moment's respects were required. 'Quite a guy, this American,' commented Danny.

'Between you and me, they want to make him a resident. Now there's a first.'

'I'd support that idea. I'd like to meet him sometime. Where does he hang out? I mean where is he living at present?'

'Where most Americans stay. In fact, it's a surprise and a pleasure for me to have an American stay here in Shiskine. Tony, that's his name, Tony stays at the hotel in Blackwaterfoot, the Kinloch hotel. Not far from here, actually.'

'Fancy that, two New Yorkers in Blackwaterfoot,' Danny said in delight at the information his evangelical hostess had shared.

'Yes indeed, oops I must scoot. The kettle will be boiled. Come down when you are ready.'

Before Danny went to bed, he examined the Carbofuran white powder. All was in order. He took the bag out of the book and placed it in the side drawer by his bed. He didn't want to carry the book around with him. Danny slept very well indeed, after a half hour drinking a mug of Ovaltine in Miss Anderson's company and discussing religion, before heading upstairs, in the almost silent pitch-black night. He heard an owl before he slept that evening and a robin's gargled tweet was heard on his windowsill, when he awoke, the following morning.

Chapter 12: The Arrest

Breakfast was a surprise. After a muesli cereal, he turned down the porridge; he welcomed a cooked breakfast which he smelt before it arrived. Bacon, two sunny side-up eggs, sausage, fried egg bread, haggis, tomato, and mushrooms lay side by side on his plate.

'I'll not need a lunch or evening meal after eating this,' he joked.

'Away with you, sir. Always a good start to the day is breakfast and at night a little light meal, for me. You can find an evening meal at the Kinloch tonight. Indeed, it's best to have all your evening meals there. They have an extensive menu.'

'Depends where I am. I might be on the other side of the island. Not sure where the most interesting birds will be.'

Danny set off on the relatively short run to Blackwaterfoot. It wasn't long before he saw the hotel and the car park. He entered the car park and turned the engine off. He lowered the sun visor as the sun shone in his eyes and thought how he could successfully kill Tony. Then he donned his deerstalker hat to complete his disguise.

Twenty minutes later Tony walked past his car and made for the front row of cars. Tony got into his silver Ford Kuga and drove out of the car park as Danny raised his phone and took a photo shot of Tony in his car and another shot as he drove off. He enlarged the photo to get its number plate: PE 18 NPN. Then it dawned on him to leave the white powder on the car door handle. He could do that at night when no-one would be around.

He sent the picture of the car to Pete in Italy with how he was going to commit the murder and he waited almost an hour before he replied.

Then he read Pete's text. 'Best plan yet. Go for it.'

He thumped the steering wheel in delight. With Tony away, he felt confident especially in his deer stalker hat, to walk along the sandy shore. He did so selecting a smooth stone from the beach, as a worry stone. He placed it in his pocket and ran his fingers over its smooth surface. He felt his worries vanish. Then he saw a golf course appear on his right. He wandered up the beach and onto the course where he watched a couple of players approach a green. He saw the second man's ball trickle into the hole, from a distance of more than 25 metres.

'Good shot sir,' Danny said to him.

'A golfer yourself?' enquired the dapper golfer in plus fours and Rupert Bear trousers with a red jumper.

'Not golf, sir. I'm a Nu Yok Yankees fan. Baseball's my sport. I'm purely a Bronx spectator of course.'

Miss Anderson liked a tidy house. She always made the beds of her guests and hoovered the carpet, each day. As she hoovered around the bed, she bumped into the side table. The jolt made the drawer open slightly. She stopped the carpet sweeper. Her inquisitiveness got the better of her. She opened the drawer further then gasped. Cocaine, she presumed. What else could it be she thought? She closed the drawer and took the hoover downstairs.

She made a cup of tea and then bowed her head in prayer asking God what she should do next.

Her response was to ring the police.

Sergeant Rory Murdoch was stirring in the milk of his Guatemalan coffee when the phone rang. He lifted it with his other hand.

'Sergeant Murdoch here. How can I help?' he said as his usual opener. Then he sipped his hot coffee.

'Oh hello. I'm Miss Ruth Anderson of the Bed and Breakfast house at Saddell View in Shiskine.'

'Ah yes, I know where you mean.'

'I'm only responding to my faith in God, but my guest, an American, has a bag of white powder. I'm sure it's cocaine. It can't be anything else. I don't want drugs in my home. Not one ounce.'

'I see. Where is he now? He's gone bird watching somewhere. He'll have to have his evening meal out, so I don't expect him back till about 8pm even 9pm.'

'Do you have his name?'

'Hold on a moment. It will be in my papers.'

Rory heard a rustling of papers grow louder as Miss Anderson approached the telephone.

'Here it is. Mr Daniel Berlotti, I think he's usually called Danny.'

'I'll have to get a warrant to search the house. Then I can come out and arrest him.'

‘Search the house? The drug is in his bedroom drawer. I have no drugs anywhere else in my property.’

‘Of course not, Miss Anderson. I wouldn’t even dream of it. I could be around by 2:30 pm. If it will be later, I’ll give you a call. Please don’t mention this to anyone yet. After all, he may be addicted to sherbet.’

‘Oh, I had not thought of that. Heaven forbid I have come to the wrong conclusion. Oh, good Lord forgive me. I might have made a grave mistake.’

‘No, you haven’t. You did the right thing to notify me. Cocaine is a class A drug. It can lead to a seven-year term of imprisonment.’

Rory took a couple of swigs of his coffee then telephoned Procurator Fiscal Fiona France at Ayr.

‘Hi Fiona. We’ve received a report of drugs at an Arran B&B. Can you arrange a warrant to search the dwelling under Section 23(3) of the Misuse of Drugs Act 1971?’

‘No problem. I’ll scan the warrant back to you. I think Sheriff Glynn is in his chambers. I’ll get it there.’

True to her word, Fiona got the document fifteen minutes later and sent it to Rory who was just taking the last dregs of his cooling coffee. Then he asked Constable Ian Steele to come with him just in case an arrest was on the cards.

It was almost 5:15pm when Rory and Ian arrived at Saddell View Guest house.

Ruth was there to greet them with a welcoming smile. ‘Welcome gents. I’ve never had a policeman visit me before you know. Far less two of you young men.’

'Yes, I know. You would be flagged up on our system if you had been reported. But goodness knows what you would be guilty of?'

Ruth took a moment to respond. 'But officer we are all guilty under God's law and we must seek his pardon.'

'Some more guilty than others and that's what we are here to investigate Miss Anderson,' said Constable Ian Steele.

'Then first a cup of tea?'

'I'd rather not,' said Constable Steele.

'And you Sergeant Murdoch?' asked Ruth.

'A coffee would do me fine,' said Rory.

Ruth froze for a moment in thought. 'You know, I've run out of coffee. It's on my shopping list for tomorrow. Danny got the last cup this morning. How silly of me. I should have got down to the Harbour Shop this afternoon. It's too late now. You see I was waiting for you to arrive.'

'I am sorry about that. We had other matters to deal with that's why we were a bit late in arriving, I'm sorry,' said Rory

'Not to worry, we can't do anything about that just now. So, let me lead you to the scene of crime as Miss Marple sometimes says,' said an impish Ruth.

The officers laughed as they made their way upstairs, their boots clattered in unison, behind Ruth's silent slippers.

'In here and that's the drawer, over there. I hope you don't mind me not opening it. I'll leave that to you. I don't want to be contaminated.'

Rory lifted the bag out with a gloved hand. He held it up to the light. 'There's something not quite right Ian.

This is either a very old cocaine sample or something quite innocent. Better get this to be analysed pronto.'

'There's no glass, blade, tin foil or any other cocaine or drug paraphernalia around,' said Ian somewhat surprised. 'Perhaps he's a dealer, certainly no heroin here.'

'I'll take a small sample. I'll leave the rest in the bag as I found it. There's doubt in my mind. It's not got all the qualities of cocaine somehow.'

'So, we take the sample back to the office to analyse it then?'

'Yup Ian.' He turned towards Ruth. 'Miss Anderson, we'll be back very quick if it is cocaine. It may on the other hand, be something quite simple and legal. So, not a word to Danny about the package, about us being here or about any suspicion when he comes back tonight. You understand?'

Danny returned at 8 pm delighted to be back in Shiskine and told Miss Anderson about his walk along the beach then a trip up to Lochranza. He ran off a dozen avian breeds from his mouth including his alleged sighting of falcons and the golden eagles. He seemed excited in relating his day while Ruth thought his rampant monologue was the effects of his morning consumption of cocaine.

At Lamlash police office the tests were finalised the following morning. Rory looked at Ian. 'It all fits together. He says he's an ornithologist. What he's doing is poisoning the birds and will sell them to taxidermists.

We banned Carbofuran years ago. That's what it is. That's his game. We got to arrest him tonight.'

As they prepared to set off to Shiskine the telephone rang. Rory reached over the desk to take the call.

'One moment sir, we have a call for you from the New York Police.'

Rory called over Ian. 'Take the other line. I guess this could be related to Danny or Tony, or any other New Yorker around.'

'Good afternoon, sir, Officer Larry Drown here. You heard of a New Yorker around Blackwaterfoot? The one who found gold and the deceased boy. Does that ring a bell?'

'You mean Tony Lupino?'

'Yes, is he still in your patch?'

'Yes, he's at the local hotel in Blackwaterfoot.'

'Can you get him on a plane back to New York, pronto?'

'Er, he's very popular here and I'm told he will be flying back soon, before Christmas. In fact, I thought you might be talking about Danny Berlotti. We are about to arrest him.'

'My God. Don't tell me Danny is on your patch? What's he done?'

'He was planning to kill raptors and have them stuffed. There's a market for that but he's using Carbofuran, the banned substance used for that illegal activity. It's an offence which carries a five-year sentence.'

'Bottom line. Arrest Danny Berlotti before he kills Tony.'

'But I don't think they've met yet. Why do you think Danny would want to kill Tony?'

'Hey, it's a long story. I'll tell you on another call. Get out and arrest Danny. Keep him in custody, for Christ's sake. Do that and I'll worry less about Tony.'

The line went dead, and Rory and Ian looked at one another.

'I don't like the way this is developing but let's get Danny first.'

It was as dark as black ink when they arrived in Shiskine. Miss Anderson rose from the table where her Bible was opened at Ephesians to let the two police officers in.

Rory put a finger to his lips. Then pointed upstairs and mouthed in a whisper: 'Is he in?'

Miss Anderson nodded her confirmation and both policemen mounted the stairs. Rory knocked on the door. 'Mr Berlotti?'

Footsteps approached the door then it opened. Danny appeared confused with a glass of beer in one hand. Both officers entered the room.

'Daniel Berlotti, you are being arrested for the possession of a controlled drug namely Carbofuran believed to be for use in killing raptors and having them stuffed. You do not have to say anything but if you do, it may be recorded and used in evidence against you. Do you understand?'

'Do I understand? What proof have you of this?'

Ian went to the drawer and opened it. There was no bag of any powder present. Danny smiled. 'I'm not sure what you are looking for.'

Ian Steele fortunately saw a strap of a bag under the bed. He bent down and lifted it up. He opened it out and saw the packet of white powder present.

'This is what we are looking for. Mr Berlotti, please turn around.' Danny complied and he was handcuffed and led downstairs. 'Let's go,' said Rory.

'But it's cocaine. It's for my private use. Is that an offence in Scotland?'

'Sir it's not cocaine. I told you, it is Carbofuran,' said Ian.

Miss Anderson remained at her table. She turned her head towards Danny as he passed her. 'Try to learn what pleases the Lord. Have nothing to do with worthless things that people do, things that belong to the darkness. Instead, bring them out to the light. And when all things are brought into the light, then their true nature is clearly revealed. Ephesians Chapter 5 verses 10-13.'

As Ruth revealed the source of her quote, the car doors closed, and the police drove Danny to Lamlash police station.

Chapter 13: Home Truths

Two days later Rory called at the hotel and asked to speak to Tony. Tony had just returned from the Harbour Shop where he had bought a copy of the local Arran Banner newspaper and spent a twenty-minute chat with Ellen, the Harbour shop owner.

'A coffee perhaps, Tony?'

Tony's eyebrows raised in harmony with a smile. 'Yes, a cappuccino at this time of the day, thanks.'

'One cappuccino and a latte please, thanks, Babs.'

'I'll bring it over in three minutes. Oh, two jam scones too?' asked the manager's wife, almost predicting the response.

'Sure thing. For us both, eh Rory,' asked Tony.

Rory nodded.

'Then make it five minutes instead,' said Babs spinning off to the kitchen with a twirl of her gaily patterned skirt.

'Well, this is a surprise meeting.'

'How true Tony. I have some information for you.'

'Information? That's interesting,' commented a slightly confused Tony.

Rory smiled at him. 'One Daniel Berlotti was arrested two days ago. He appeared at Ayr sheriff court this morning and was remanded in custody pending a trial in a few weeks.'

Tony smacked his forehead and his mouth opened finding no words to speak at first. 'Good grief. Daniel! What the hell is he doing here? What have you charged him with?' asked Tony leaning forward not to miss a single word.

'Possession of Carbofuran with intent of injuring wildlife.'

'Wildlife? What the heck was Danny up to? He knows nothing about wildlife or nature, absolutely zilch.'

'I don't know but the substance is banned here. It's toxic, you know.'

There was a silence in which they accepted the tray of coffees and scones which arrived. They both took a sip of their coffees as they made sense of the happenings.

'So Tony, how do you know Danny?'

'I've got a few days left. Perhaps it's time to tell you exactly what's true and what's not. Danny is the brother of Mario I got imprisoned for life. Danny's father was gunned down in the Bronx in broad daylight. A Mafia boss who killed or had killed some twelve people over his rule in the same district.'

'But that's the law. He shouldn't have had a grudge against you?'

'Rory, my own father was gunned down. He was a Mafia boss, as well.'

`You mean you are in the Mafia too?' asked Rory with increasing interest stemming from disbelief and now anxiety.

'No, I'm the first generation to get out of it. I wanted to clear up the scandals. I prosecute Mafia folk and sure make many enemies.'

'I'm sure you would. A dangerous lifestyle, I am sure.'

'Yes, and you being a policemen recognise the situation I was in. Before I left Nu Yok I cited Danny for two murders. I heard he went missing, underground more likely. But the NYPD, err... the Nu Yok Police, gave me secret houses to live in. I was sometimes moved twice a month to somewhere new. I was driven in unmarked police cars to work and returned home by leaving different doors to find the driver to take me home. It was an insane lifestyle. The more Mafia I put behind bars the more I was a wanted man. A wanted dead man.'

'God America. It could only happen there, I guess,' said Rory.

'Yep, and I cracked. I had to get a break. I had to get away from this madness before me. So, when they came to take me to work, I was not there. I was at Kennedy Airport with a ticket to Glasgow and a booked car to travel to Arran,' said Tony with a satisfied look on his face.

'And may I ask. Alban Caskie, did he exist? Were you really his relative?'

Tony's head lowered and he grunted. 'I had hoped that question would never be asked. I have no Sioux blood or connection with the Red Indian tribes and as for Alban Caskie, well; he was a figure of my imagination.'

'I've not told you the whole truth, Tony. I heard from a transatlantic call from the NYPD. The gold nuggets were stolen from Levi's Emporium in 1932. It's still a Manhattan business and they want the gold nuggets returned.'

'That's news to me. Had I known, I'd have returned the gold to them. It means the gold will have to be released from Edinburgh and returned to New York. I can live with that but am sorry for the students, the gold diggers and the fact the gold brought Arran no wealth.'

Several moments elapsed as Tony wondered what else Rory might spring on him while Rory wondered at what pace he should spill the beans.

'The plane?'

'No not Sioux intuition. Just potluck. I was there at the right time. No more, no less. That's in the hands of those history folk at Glasgow University and that's fine by me.'

'Finally, Tony. Callum. How did you really find him?'

'I'm sure I told you. I've had kids go astray reported and they have been found near or in water. It's a fascination for them. In summer there would have been few deaths but whatever took him to the loch in early winter, was not a rational decision. He just had to be there, after you had completed the door-to-door enquiries.'

Rory finished his latte. 'So, what will you do now?'

'I'd like to get to Ayr and see the trial. Oh, and one thing I beg of you Rory. Don't break the hearts of the local people. I meant no harm to them.'

'You say, Daniel Berlotti is in the Mafia and has no interests in ornithology?'

Tony laughed. He shook his head. 'Daniel an ornithologist? Don't make me laugh louder.'

'Okay but has he a role in the Mafia?'

'He sure does. You know the ranks of the Mafia?

'Can't say I do, Tony.'

'Well, the Boss is the undisputed leader of the family. He makes all the decisions and gets a share of all the profits. My father was a Boss, the Godfather. The Underboss is the second in command in the family and 'heir' to the throne. That's where Daniel comes in. The Consigliere. ...well, he's an advisor to the Boss and resolves disputes in the family. Then you get the capos, the foot soldiers that carry out the dirty work and the associates. They are all part of the family. That's how it is, and they get into rackets galore be it cars, trade unions, drugs, service industries and even politics. Mark my words Rory, you just don't wanna mix with the Mafia.'

'Tony, I think I know what's going to happen. You'll likely hear from the procurator fiscal before too long.'

Tony took a walk along the Blackwaterfoot beach aware his story was coming apart. But he felt sure he could be forgiven. He stopped and looked out onto the shores of the Kintyre peninsula. A quiet land with sensible, solid folk just like those on Arran. There was nowhere in America like that these days. Then his thoughts turned towards Daniel, his cousin. What the hell was he doing with poison? Perhaps he was the one who he had in mind. But how did he know where he was? How did he know I was at Blackwaterfoot?

He turned back and as he was approaching the hotel, he noticed three cyclists checking their bikes. He approached them.

'Hi guys. Hope no punctures,' said Tony almost feigning concern.

'Naw, just checkin' tyre pressure and makin' sure thirs nae glass or nails in the tyres.'

One of the cyclists approached Tony. 'Are you Tony Lupino, by any chance?'

'I sure am. And who are you, may I ask,' he said with a smile.

'We're fae Glasca on a weekend ride aroond Arran. Bit my brother married an American and lives upstate New York.'

'Not so far away from me then?'

'Aye, a suppose not. But Billy, mi brither sent me a text and said I might find you at Blackwaterfoot. Find the gold finder, the discoverer of a Nazi plane and the missin' boy.'

Tony looked puzzled. His eyebrows gathered. 'How does your brother know so much about me?'

The cyclist leant his bike beside the wall of the hotel and produced his phone.

'Look at this. Here's the newspaper article. I think it's the New York Times.'

Tony took the phone and enlarged the article. He saw the newspaper date was over a week ago. Plenty time for Daniel to get to Blackwaterfoot with the poison, and no, not a bird twitcher, but a potential murderer and he was to be his victim.

He handed the phone back with a worried look. 'Thanks, that's most interesting,' he said and turned away towards the hotel and his room. The cyclists looked at each other in bewilderment.

'Strange fella,' said one cyclist and the other two nodded in agreement.

Rory sat on his bed and wondered how his encounters recorded in the Arran Banner had sped to New York so quickly then he assumed a stringer in New York had filed copy of Hugh's article. And so, The New York Times learned of his activities. Tony was not pleased when he Googled the New York News in his bedroom. Indeed, his life on Arran was there for all to read. His adversaries might be unlikely to read The New York Times but word would get to them. He felt sure about that, and it made him feel very uncomfortable indeed.

The very next day, 1st December, he received a citation to attend Ayr Sheriff court on 19th December to be a witness in the case against Daniel Berlotti. 19th December. He was booked to fly back to New York on that date.

He phoned the American Embassy to explain why he needed an extension to his visa. They asked him to scan the citation to them and they would resolve the situation, as soon as possible.

Indeed, later that day they rang him back to give him an extension and requested him to contact them once the trial had concluded.

Chapter 14: A Call From The States

Rory stretched back with his hands behind his head. He looked up at his office clock realising 5 pm was three minutes away. Already he had switched off for the day. Then he stood up to take his empty coffee cup back to the kitchen. As he did so, he heard a phone call being received in the front office. He squirted some washing up liquid into the plastic white bowl and immersed his mug. As he turned on the hot water, his secretary, Rosie, entered the kitchen.

'Rory, I'll put this call through to you. It's from New York. No kidding. I loved his accent.'

Rory sighed. This call would delay his departure. He dried his hands on the kitchen towel and returned to his seat preparing for the call to be transferred. He had no idea what the call would be about. To put him at ease, Rosie shouted through.

'A Guatemalan for you, perhaps?' she asked almost knowing his response.

Rory's eyes lit up. 'Yes, I've a feeling I might need one right now.'

The call came through to his office. Rory placed his hand on the receiver and after a deep breath lifted it.

'Good afternoon. Sergeant Rory Murdoch here. How can I help you?'

'Gee I guess you must be packing up soon. You are five hours ahead of us. I've just had a fried baloney sandwich with a coke for lunch, so I'm ready to go. Are you?'

'It's good to hear a police colleague's voice from so far away. Yes, I'm certainly ready and interested to hear what you have to say.'

The New York policeman laughed. 'Sure, like that accent, Bud. I mean Rory.'

'Fire away.'

'Okay, I'm Officer Luc Lombardo, Fifth quarter New York Police. I wanna pick your brains.'

'Pick my brains? I've a rural patch compared with you. I can't imagine our police work could be more dissimilar.'

'Okay let's see. Do you know Danny Zesnick?'

Rory shook his head. The question was not difficult to answer.

'No, never heard of him.'

'Okay what about Larry Oblinski ?'

Rory smiled as his Guatemalan coffee appeared. He stirred it with a teaspoon. What names these Americans had.

'No, I've never been to America. Don't know that name either.'

There was a moment's pause. Rory sipped his coffee. He wondered how many more names Luc Lombardo would have to go through before he gave up.

'What about Tony Lupino?' asked Luc as he combed his hair with the fingers of his left hand.

Rory almost gulped his next sip. Tony, New York, police, he thought to himself. 'Tony Lupino. He's at Blackwaterfoot. Remarkable guy. There are some who want to give him a civic honour, I've heard.'

'Yeah, popular?'

Rory scratched the back of his head. 'Yes, very popular. He found the body of a missing youth, made a few correct predictions, located a WWII Nazi plane and found gold in one of the remote areas of the island.'

'You know much about the guy?' asked Luc.

'I guess not too much. He arrived unannounced. Only the hotel knew he was coming.'

'And Sioux chief?'

Rory hesitated. He did not want the islanders to feel stupid.

'He said he was a direct descendant of a Blackwaterfoot man, Alban Caskie. Goes a long way back.'

'Yeah? '

Rory tried to detect the caller's expression.

'Tony will have no Arran blood in him. He's of Mafia red blood stock.'

'The Mafia! Well, I did not see that coming. He's done more good than anything else here. That stretches my imagination.'

'His uncle, Ricardo Penachio, was gunned down in the Bronx. Left his fortune to Tony's father. Tony's father Carlo Barcurio, was found in the Patchogue river in New York, bullet to his head, face down in the cold water.'

'Er...let me think. Tony Lupino's father was Carlo Barcurio, Mafia, right?'

'Dat's right. Tony changed his name to Lupino. That's his latest name. It was Larry Oblinski and Danny Zesnick before. He changes his name regularly. He has to.'

'I see,' said Rory digesting the information at the pace of a limping dog.

'Tony was just five years of age when his father died. He grew up detesting the Mafia. He studied hard at school. He became a lawyer, a good one too. He is a prosecutor; the NYPD like him.'

'Okay, but I can't see where this is going?' asked Rory with his coffee mug half empty.

'Tony prosecutes many Mafia men. He is detested by them, so we gave him 24 hr security, witness protection by any other name. We drove him to his work, had armed guards at court and he had to tell us where he was going if at work outside court or on a social engagement. He breached the arrangement. He's still a wanted man by the Mafia. Mind you he seems safe where he is, on Arran, now.'

'So, he's been on this witness protection arrangement for some time?'

'He sure has. But we traced him here.'

'Umm...but no crime has been committed.'

There was a lacuna. 'Not as simple. His father inherited some gold from his uncle, and we believe it's now in Tony's hands.'

'Ah,' said Rory pleased at last to share some of his intelligence, 'the gold is not with Tony now.'

'You mean he sold it on Arran?'

'No, I suspect he planted the gold and the University of Glasgow archaeologists found it. It's in safe hands now. In Edinburgh they are working on who it belongs to.' Tony took the last dregs of his coffee and wondered if another nugget could appear. Then he remembered the time. His secretary had gone home. 'Okay, so has he got a criminal record?'

'Criminal record? No, he just ain't got one.'

There was a silence during which Rory wondered why there was a telephone call in the first place. Luc detected his mind.

'It's the gold. His uncle's gold.'

'But if his father inherited it, Tony wasn't receiving stolen goods, as such.'

'The gold nuggets were stolen from Levi's Emporium in 1932. It's still a Manhattan business and they want the gold nuggets returned.'

'Yeah, I heard that. It will be heading back to New York as soon as they have finished with it in Edinburgh.' Rory nodded his head slowly in satisfaction. The purpose of the call was plane to him now.

'He's on a three-month visitor's visa,' informed Rory.

'When does that expire?'

'19th December.'

'Okay, you let me know his flight details and we'll pick him up,' Luc said.

'Might be a bit later. He's a witness in Danny's court case.'

'Er...that should be good. That is as long as Danny gets a prison sentence.'

A silent nod of agreement crossed Rory's face.

'So, you will pick him up to interview him?'

'Yes, see why he jumped protection and get them gold nuggets back to where they belong,' said Luc tweaking his cheek.

The call concluded smartly. Rory felt a need to speak to Tony and remind him some home truths. But it was possibly best to let him see out his stay first.

Rory advised Alan Dunbar his DI in Ayr of the transatlantic call the following morning.

'Best not upset the apple cart or the grateful community,' was his response. 'Let him see out the court case, yeah agreed.'

Rory smiled. Things were falling into place, as long as the court procedures went the predicted way.

Chapter 15: Fair View Hotel

Tony stayed at the Fair View hotel where Karen and Vince Dean were the hosts. They had read about Tony's remarkable life on Arran in the Ayr Advertiser and Tony prepared to keep up his pretence to perfection. This was not the time to shed his load of deception.

'It must have been so rewarding to find you had a relative in Blackwaterfoot, Tony,' said Karen as she drew back the curtains in the empty lounge, at night.

'It was the Sioux who told me about him, and the research followed at Columbia University in Manhattan. They have a great library. And yes, you can imagine how pleased I was to have a long-lost Scottish background.'

'I'm interested in the gold you found too. Do you think there's much more to find?' asked Vince as he passed by his table still holding his Arsenal programme from when they played and beat Aston Villa last week.

'I'd be a very wealthy man if I knew. But the signs are there. They have already found gold in Argyll and it was found in a very remote part of Arran, not so far away from the mainland or too dissimilar in land formation from the find in Argyll.'

Vince nodded his understanding.

'We must not keep you up all night. Will you be the first witness in the case tomorrow?' asked Karen.

'No, I'm second or third I think the procurator fiscal told me. Definitely not the first.'

Staying at the Fair View Hotel meant a gentle stroll to the Sheriff Court at Ayr, which was situated very near the lengthy golden sands where dogs teased the approaching dribbling waves. On at least two occasions, Tony saw horses gallop in the sea, three metres from the shore.

Chapter 16: Ayr Sheriff Court, December 19th

Sheriff A.G. Moffat strode up to his lofted seat on the bench as the ex-marine court official shouted for the court to order and to rise.

When all had settled down, the Sheriff eyed all fifteen members of the jury. The eyes of each jury person had their eyes on him too.

'Madam Prosecutor, the case please,' he said with a nod to Miss Fiona France.

Fiona stood up pushing her chair behind her with a shunt from her calves.

'My Lords, this is a case of the accused being in possession of an illegal substance namely Carbofuran. Mr Daniel Berlotti is charged under Section 11, Schedule 6 of the Wildlife and Countryside Act 1981. I have a duty to inform the jury what this substance is and will now do so if the court allows.'

Sheriff Moffat nodded his approval as clearly he was as keen to discover what the banned substance was, as each member of the jury.

'Carbofuran is currently the toxic substance most used by bird poisoners. From 2002 to 2011, there were 633 confirmed bird-poisoning incidents in the UK, of which 316 cases—50%—involved carbofuran. Carbofuran, which is marketed under the trade name Furadan, is a carbonate insecticide, and its approval for use as such, was withdrawn in the UK in 2001. There is therefore no legal purpose for which anyone might possess carbofuran in the UK. Carbofuran is especially toxic to birds, and a very small amount indeed would kill a large bird of prey such as a golden eagle by breaking down its central nervous system. On Arran there are several pairs of Golden Eagles in the north of the island. Carrion-feeding raptors are especially susceptible to Carbofuran poisoning, where the poison is administered via laced bait. A gamekeeper who was convicted of poisoning birds of prey in Skibo, Scotland, in 2011 was found to possess 10 kilograms of carbofuran, which would have been sufficient to kill every bird of prey in the UK. Bird poisoners are clearly targeting a range of birds of prey. The RSSPB's Bird crime 2010 lists poisoning cases involving 20 red kites, 30 buzzards, two goshawks, eight peregrines, five golden eagles, one white-tailed eagle and one sparrow hawk, and 36 of those poisoning cases in 2010 involved carbofuran. Figure 2, which I provide as production 1, sets out the number of confirmed cases of bird of prey poisoning over the past decade, showing the species that were targeted and the extent to which those cases involved Carbofuran. It is such a dangerous substance that it can cause the death of anyone who comes into contact with it when it enters their body.' Fiona then gave this summary of the substance to the defence lawyer who gave it a cursory glance. He had already taken a note of her verbal delivery.

'Are you now ready to call your first witness?' asked the Sheriff.

Fiona called for Miss Ruth Anderson. The court official shouted her name immediately afterwards and having heard her name being called twice, Ruth's steps quickened, and she was still at that pace as she approached the witness box. She carefully gathered the Bible in both of her hands. Then she opened the sacred book just to check she was about to take an oath on a real bible.

That formal procedure over, the first question was asked.

'Please, you may put the Bible down now, the oath has been made,' suggested Fiona kindly.

Ruth looked perturbed. 'If you don't mind, I'd like to hold it through my evidence.'

Fiona looked up at the Sheriff so he could decide on the matter.

'Very well Miss Anderson, as long as you don't leave with it,' he said with a grin.

'Oh, I'd not do that, Sir. The Bible has a very important place in the court system.'

'I shall proceed,' said Fiona recognising a potentially difficult witness. 'Tell the court your full name and age please.'

Ruth gasped. 'My name is Ruth Mary Anderson, and I am in my sixties.'

Fiona's eyes stared at Ruth. 'Is that 61 or 69 perhaps?'

'If you must know, the good Lord has spared me 68 years of life so far.'

'Thank you, Miss Anderson. I remind you accuracy is required in your evidence as in all cases too. Now you live on Arran, at Saddell View Guesthouse, at Shiskine. Is that so?'

'Yes, that is so.'

'Recently you had a male guest. Do you see him in court this morning?'

'Yes, I have seen him.'

'Can I ask you to point him out, for clarity?'

'Must I?'

'Yes, you must,' said Fiona abruptly, frustrated at Miss Anderson's prevarication.

'Very well, it's that man there wearing a rather loud shirt, I am sure you agree. But of course, he is American. A New York resident in fact, I noted his address in the visitor's book in the lounge, first. You see when he first spoke on the phone, I thought he might be a Canadian.'

'Your duties at the guest house will be to prepare the bedding each day, especially if you have a guest spending a few days in your home. Not so?'

'That is true. I suppose you want to know what I saw?'

'Indeed, Miss Anderson but from the very beginning. What did you do on that particular morning?'

'I did what I do every morning. I get out of bed and say my prayers kneeling by my bed. That's usually at 6 am. Then I have a shower dress and read the Bible. I'm reading it through from start to finish.'

'From Mathew to Revelations, you mean, Miss Anderson?' asked the Sheriff.

'Good heavens no. That's only the New Testament. You would miss out the wonderful Song of Songs and the marvellous book of Proverbs if you missed out the Old Testament. I'm currently at The Consecration of the Alter at Chapter 43 verse 18 of the book of Ezekiel.'

'I feel we're digressing. Can I bring you to the point you entered Mr Berlotti's room that morning,' asked Fiona, with an audible sigh.

Ruth cleared her throat. 'Yes, I had a duster with me, and I polished the mirror and made his bed. It was when I was around the left side of the bed; the carpet sweeper knocked the bedside tabletop drawer open. I noticed the top drawer was ever so slightly open, rather. I thought it strange that his handkerchief was in a plastic bag. But in fact, it wasn't a hanky. It really wasn't.' Ruth looked at the high roof of the court and kept her stare there as she spoke. 'Heavens above, may the good Lord forgive my first thought, but I presumed the white powder was cocaine. And it had entered my home. God forgive me for allowing this to happen.'

'You thought it was cocaine. So, what did you do next?'

'Well, I opened the drawer further. I saw it was a medium sized bag but the white stuff, did not fill it. It seemed to be about, well let me think... around four tablespoons of the powder, I'd say.'

'And what action did you take then.'

'My thoughts were in a muddle. I could return the bag and say nothing, but I did not feel the Lord would agree. So, I telephoned the police station at Lamlash. I spoke to Sergeant Rory Murdoch. He's our community policemen and I would think he had come across cocaine. I mean, not him in a personal way. I mean some of the younger folk take cocaine, I think. Although I'd never seen anyone take it myself.'

'And did Sergeant Murdoch do anything else?' asked Fiona.

'Yes, he came to my home, and I offered him a cup of tea. But he preferred coffee, but I did not have any. I don't drink coffee myself, you see. So, we went into Mr Berlotti's room, and he took a sample of the white stuff. I remember he told me it was not like the cocaine he had seized before, and I suggested it might be baking powder.'

'But it wasn't baking powder, was it?'

'That's right. The Sergeant even thought it could even be sherbet,' said Ruth, smiling, almost bursting into a giggle. 'My instinct was in fact right. I was told after they arrested my guest that it was a substance banned in the country. I forget its name. It was something beginning with C, I remember,' she said wringing her hands together till her knuckles turned white.

'Thank you, Miss Anderson, I have no further questions, but stay where you are, Mr George Sinclair has a few questions for you.'

'Thank you Miss France. I look forward to meeting Mr St Clair. St. Clare of Assisi is the patron saint of televisions and computer screens, believe it or not. An early follower of St. Francis, Clare, founded The Order of Poor Ladies, which eventually became known as the Poor Clares.'

'Mr Sinclair, the witness is yours,' said Fiona sitting down as she threw her pen to the desk.

George Sinclair was a thin but tall man whose string maroon and white striped tie was loosely tied. His suit was navy blue as fitted the court's approval but his men's Oxford dress periwinkle shoes, out of sight, showed him to be a man of style, but perhaps not in the current vogue of fashion. He stood up at a slow rate as if a mug of coffee was being poured gently.

'Good morning, Miss Anderson. Remember the Lord has chosen the righteous, for his own. The Psalms chapter 4 verse 3.'

Ruth smiled. 'The Lord is in his holy temple; he has his throne in heaven. He watches people everywhere and knows what they are doing. The Psalms chapter 11 verse....'

Sheriff Moffat was uncomfortable moving around on his chair. He needed to bring the case to the fore. He interrupted Ruth.

'This is a court of Law, I remind you. Not a church of worship. Can we agree not to stray from the case? Can we ask the Lord to watch over us and not intervene?' There was total silence in the court for a few moments. 'Mr Sinclair, please continue.'

'Miss Alexander. Your guest, Mr Berlotti. He's American, not so?'

'From New York,' she said.

'And you had no misgivings in taking him in as your guest?'

'None whatsoever, except...'

Mr Sinclair looked up at Ruth. 'Except?'

'Yes, he did not like to eat porridge. He wanted two eggs sunny side up with some rashers of bacon for breakfast and a cup of strong black tea. It took me by surprise, especially the tea, but he is American, you know?'

'And you went up into his room as you told the court. What right did you have to open his bedside drawer?'

'It was partially open. I was initially pleased. I had placed a Gideon's Bible there, but it was the flash of white which attracted me, after I accidentally bumped the drawers with the carpet sweeper.'

'Nevertheless, you took possession of his property without his permission.'

Ruth cleared her dry throat. A court usher brought a glass of cold water to her aid. She thanked him and drank the whole glass in one go. 'Indeed, I did. I asked the Lord if I was doing the right thing and I was encouraged to make further enquiry. I suspected it was cocaine and that was an offence. Cocaine in my house? God forbid. That is an affront to the Lord.'

'But it was not cocaine. It was baking soda, wasn't it? Your second thought, more realistic, I suggest?'

Ruth's eyes darted around the court. Was this a trick question, she wondered?

'Yes, baking soda was my second thought and that was a surprised he had that, although he told me he always enjoyed cooking. But Sergeant Murdoch informed me it was in fact an illegal substance and poisonous too. Con...something, I really can't quite remember what it was.'

'My client is a keen ornithologist. Did he tell you that?'

'Er... yes he was. He always went out in the morning, and he came home usually around 9 pm. You see I don't provide evening meals.'

`Not only ornithology but finding the fauna and flora of a new country. A real holiday break on Arran. Is Arran not a popular tourist island?'

'Oh yes, it is. Mind you not so many come in late autumn, early winter. It gets dark early. It picks up at Christmas of course, but yes, tourism is the main er..main earner for the local economy.'

'So, an American, keen to see the winter array of birds in a new country. Not unusual I'd say?'

'No, but I've never had a New Yorker before. I've had Americans but never a New Yorker, and someone here to study birds in winter, is not so common. They usually come to golf, to go on walks, go to the island's many beaches, sail their yachts, that sort of pursuit. Usually when the weather is better.'

'So, Miss Anderson, he was not a usual winter guest. So why try and get him prosecuted for being a bird watcher? I have no further questions. You may now leave the witness box,' he said and promptly sat down beside his client.

'But you asked a question. Do you not want to know that I suspected an illegal substance and Sergeant Murdoch agreed with me? I can face the Lord with an honest heart, at last now.'

'Thank you, Miss Anderson, as you have been told, you may now leave the court,' said Sheriff Moffat with a very relieved smile.

'But it's my resident who is on trial. Can I not be allowed to watch the case unfold to its conclusion? I mean it may possibly have only been sherbet, after all.'

Danny nodded ostentatiously so everyone could conclude he had a sweet tooth.

'You are quite right. Of course, you can. You must sit in the public gallery and stay silent. You understand?' asked the Sheriff.

Ruth knew her time at the witness box was over. As she left the stand, she patted the Bible which lay on a shelf below the witness's rail.

'I call upon Sergeant Murdoch,' announced Fiona with a sigh of relief and a smile as wide as Ayr's sandy beach.

Rory strode confidently into the witness box as he had done many times in the past. His involvement would be brief, and he knew there was still time to secure a good coffee after his questioning. His almost perfunctory oath was taken.

'Officer, you name rank and length of police service, please.' Fiona asked aware the words came to her without much thought.

'Sergeant Rory Anderson Murdoch. I have been a police officer for thirty-one years, based at Lamlash on Arran.'

'Just a point of clarification, officer. Your middle name. Are you a relative of the previous witness?'

Rory's smirk of a smile was noted by all around the court. 'Miss Anderson?' Rory asked.

'Yes, Miss Anderson,' responded Fiona.

'Anderson is not an uncommon name, even on the island but I regret to inform you I am in no way related to Miss Ruth Anderson.'

'Thank you, officer. Now I turn to the case. You were called to the guest house of Miss Anderson. What did you find when you got there?'

'I was taken up to the guestroom of Mr Daniel Berlotti. I was reliably informed that Mr Berlotti was out, but Miss Anderson was anxious to expedite my visit.'

'And what did you find in the bedroom?'

'I was directed to the bedside table in which there was a bag of what seemed to be white powder. Miss Anderson thought it might be cocaine or baking powder, but I took a small sample of the white substance for analysis, leaving the bag in the drawer.'

'And where was the analysis done?'

'It was done at the Lamlash office where a civilian crime analyst, Catherine Moir, had arrived from the mainland to determine its nature.'

'And what was her report?'

'I have her written report with me,' said Rory handing the paper to Fiona who looked at it briefly then flew it over the table into the hands of Mr Sinclair, who studied it in detail.

'It shows the banned substance to be the illegal poison, Carbofuran.'

'And what had this substance been used for before it was banned, Mr Murdoch?'

'It was used in the taxidermy industry. The substance is used to kill raptors and wild animals by poisoning them.'

'And what risk does it have for its human users?'

'It is highly toxic and is likely to kill anyone who handles it and especially if it enters his or her body through any orifice. '

'And why was it banned?'

'Because it led to painful deaths of raptors, and it was a poisonous toxin which had little other use in society.'

'What was your next action?'

'Along with Officer Steele, we returned in the early evening and arrested Mr Berlotti and charged him under

Section 11, Schedule 6 of the Wildlife and Countryside Act 1981. He was subsequently detained at Lamlash police station then transferred to the police station here at Ayr.'

'Did Mr Berlotti at any point state where the substance had been obtained?'

'He did tell me it was cocaine from a man he met in Glasgow on his way to Arran, but no name was forthcoming, and he had trouble indicating the location where such an exchange was said to have taken place. I did have a telephone call from the New York Police, and they told me that Mr Lupino was....'

'Objection. This is hearsay evidence,' said Mr Sinclair jumping to his feet in anticipation of damming evidence for his client.

'Mr Murdoch such evidence is hearsay as you should know,' stated the sheriff.

'I apologise.'

'Thank you Sergeant Murdoch, I have no other questions,' said Fiona brushing over the objection.'

'Mr Sinclair,' invited the sheriff.

Mr Sinclair pulled his slipped gown over his shoulders as he stood up. 'Officer Murdoch. I put it to you that my client could have had no idea what the substance was.'

'Then I would suggest he was very unwise to obtain such a dangerous substance without knowing its nature?'

'Maybe he thought it was social cocaine?'

'Social cocaine? I am not familiar with that term.'

'Then let me clarify, perhaps he thought it was for his personal use, as is common I believe in the south of

England where even learned Judges and senior police officers are known to consume this drug.'

'Mr Sinclair, this court sits in Scotland and acts under Scottish legal statutes. I would be interested to learn who you are referring to in my chambers at a later time.'

'I shall be happy to inform you of the popular current uses of the cocaine drug's use in the UK and by film stars too. But if it was cocaine and Miss Anderson is neither of the teenage years of experimentation and her faith does not allow her body to consume any drug, was it not natural for Mr Berlotti to hide the substance, as a precaution. Not so?'

'That may well be the case.'

'And you approve of people entering the possessions of another without permission?' asked the defence agent.

'I assure you, although the drawer was only slightly ajar, Miss Anderson did nothing wrong in making her discovery and subsequent report to myself.'

'I put it to you that my client is a keen bird watcher on the beautiful island of Arran and his private use of cocaine offended no-one. It hardly makes for a good relationship in the American tourist market, if an over-zealous housekeeper challenges an American visitor on such speculation, does it?'

'Speculation it may have been, but she was right to report a dangerous toxic matter in her house.'

'I have no further questions Mr Murdoch.'

And as Mr Sinclair returned to his seat, he lifted his pen and was seen to make copious notes. But was that for the benefit of his client or a piece of judicial showmanship? The jury must have had mixed feelings.

'I call upon Mr Tony Lupino,' Fiona announced as her next witness approached the bench.

Daniel looked up at him briefly then down at his feet. His frown showed his contempt for the family witness.

Tony took the oath, and the usher removed the Bible.

'Please tell the court your name, age and profession.'

'I am Tony Lupino aged fifty-three. I am from Nu Yok, and I am a District attorney. That would make me a procurator fiscal, if I worked in Scotland. Our roles are similar, though the legislation differs.'

Fiona smiled at the thought he could have been a colleague had he settled in Ayrshire. 'Mr Lupino, do you recognise the accused?'

'Yes, he's my cousin.'

There was a titter amongst the public. But Fiona seemed to carry on as if nothing could stop her flow.

'Why did you decide to spend a winter holiday in Scotland and in particular on Arran?'

Tony straightened his tie looked up at the Sheriff briefly and then at Fiona.

'There is some background to my life I must state at the outset. My father and generations before him were members of a Nu Yok Mafia family.'

There was a gasp in the court and the journalists recording the case for their papers perked up their interest having heard Tony's statement.

'My father and Daniel's father were brothers, both men were killed in Nu York by another Mafia family, the Barbieri. That was the final straw. I decided to be a prosecutor and I specialised in taking Mafia cases to court but first I changed my name to Tony Lupino, a surname with no Mafia connection. In the course of my work, I prosecuted Daniel's brother, Mario. He received twenty-two years for the murder of Antonio Barbieri. Paulo Barberi received twenty-six years for the murder of my uncle's nephew, Luca, and I had recently charged my cousin Daniel, with the murder of two youths, Flavio and Stephano Lastra. That case caused friction in the family, but I was determined to rid Nu Yok of its entire Mafia links.'

'Is that possible to prosecute a family member?'

'They are no longer my family. They remain in the other family, the Mafia. Our surnames are different; no one suspected we were related. Anyway, the decision rests with the jury. I give them the case to decide. However, the NYPD, the Nu Yok Police department, came to me and expressed their concern about my negative relationship with Mafia members. Their solution was dramatic. I was to be given strict police supervision.'

Fiona looked puzzled. She nodded to her witness to continue.

'I was brought to court each day in an unmarked police car and driven home to a new home every two weeks. I was not allowed out of the house unless I told the police where I was going and even then, I had an armed police officer escort on every outing. This lasted all though the previous year and up to September this year. That was when I decided to get out, have a break and relax.'

'I see and understand. But why come to Blackwaterfoot?'

'I had inherited some gold nuggets. I wondered how to get rid of them. I thought perhaps I could find an ideal rural community and searched an atlas. I found the Scottish islands were all a possibility but the voyage to Arran was the shortest and so I decided to go there.'

'The gold nuggets?' asked Fiona.

'On an Arran map, I guessed the northwest was the most remote. I'd secreted the gold there but had to have a plan for the community to find them. I had six nuggets and I gave one to Robbie Crawford, the manager at the hotel. He knew the ropes I didn't. It was the west coast of Arran not the wild west. He informed the police and they had to find out the source and the quality of the gold. But anyway, I gave them the location and sure enough the rest of the gold was found.'

'Am I right to think you gained nothing from this act?'

'No nothing material but I gained a free conscience as I had got rid of the Mafia gold.'

'Where is the gold now?'

'It's in Edinburgh, awaiting its final movement back to Levi's Emporium in Nu Yok from where it was stolen many years ago.'

Fiona shuffled her papers.

'The Nazi plane. Explain that Mr Lupino.'

'That was my downfall. I had no idea a plane was there. I just walked around in that desolate part of the island to relax and noticed a land elevation. When I got closer, I realised I had found an old plane. I scraped off the mud from its wing and found a swastika. I had to think what to do with this find. It was too much to tackle by one man, so I alerted the police, and they created a cordon around the area as they expected visitors to the site. But historians and archaeologists from Glasgow

University came. Bomb disposal army people came to defuse its unexploded bomb too. The plane was eventually uncovered and transported to the mainland. The remains of the crew were given to the German Embassy in London.'

'You said your downfall?'

'Yes, the gold was minor news, but the gold and the aircraft find, attracted much media coverage. I learned it had gotten to the Nu Yok Times and so Daniel knew I was on Arran.'

'And the significance of that?'

'Well, my life would be at risk. I planned to make a hasty retreat to Nu Yok. Especially when I discovered he had been charged with the offence he finds facing today in court.'

'About your cousin. Did he always have an interest in ornithology?'

Tony's laugh quickly disintegrated into a broad smile. 'Never have I heard of him talk about that. Nu Yok is not the place to see birds other than blackbirds and pigeons. I guess he might not even have heard of the word ornithology.'

Mr Sinclair stood up, like a jack in the box. 'Objection my Lord, that's pure speculation. He is making my client seem simple as well.'

'Yes, objection sustained. The jury will make no assumption Mr Berlotti has no understanding of the word ornithology. Please continue Miss France.'

Fiona turned over a page of her notes.

'If Mr Berlotti is not an ornithologist and we have identified the white substance as Carbofuran, a toxic poison. Can you suggest what use Mr Berlotti could possibly have for his possession of the drug?'

'First you must assess why two relatives independently make their way not just to Arran but Blackwaterfoot in particular, in mid-winter. The likelihood of that happening I suggest is significant. That I had charged Daniel Berlotti with two murders is an even more significant factor as Daniel's brother is serving a 24-year sentence. And given that he was in possession of a toxic substance, I suggest that is tantamount to attempted murder and the prosecutor might wish to consider that as an additional charge.'

'Thank you Mr Lupino. Indeed, I would alert the court to an amendment to the charge which alters the *nomen juris* to a double charge, the *mens rae*, being attempted murder of Mr Lupino,' said Helen.

There was a moment's silence as the Sheriff considered her application. He wrote copiously in his folder then placed his pen down before him. 'In the light of the evidence heard, I will hear the attempted murder charge,' he said, and the jury looked more solemn by the second.

'Mr Lupino, I have no further questions,' said Fiona with a grin more than a smile at Tony. Then she turned to the sheriff.

'My Lord that is the case for the prosecution.'

Mr Sinclair stood to inform the court that he had no further questions for Mr Lupino but stated his intentions too.

'I move to bring my client to the witness box.'

Daniel Berlotti looked like a frightened rabbit as he approached the witness box despite being forewarned it was his best defence, by Mr Sinclair. He grabbed the witness rail as if it was a stuttering bus running out of fuel.

He was given the Bible and swore to tell the truth.

'Mr Berlotti, how long have you been an ornithologist?'

'Just over a year.'

'And tell the court why you came to Arran?'

'I learned that there were a few Golden Eagles. I hoped to get a good photo of at least one of them.'

'Did you know your cousin was on Arran too?'

'No, that was a complete surprise,' he lied.

'How did you arrive? Was it a trip from New York to Glasgow?'

'No. I went via Kenya. I thought as I was going so far west, I'd visit my relative in Nairobi. I had not seen him for a few years.'

'So, New York to Kenya and Kenya to Scotland, the journey of a holiday maker.'

'Exactly.'

'But when you got to Glasgow you were confronted by a local youth. What happened there?'

'He sold me some cocaine. He told me it was pure, and I bought a bag of it. I use cocaine in the States. In Nu Yok, the police turn a blind eye to cocaine consumption but if that is not the law in Scotland, well I admit I bought cocaine for my personal use.'

'The evidence shows that it was not cocaine. It was Carbofuran. How did you feel about that?'

'Diddled.'

There was a murmur of sniggers on hearing he had been 'diddled'.

There followed a minor disturbance in the court as a secretary arrived bringing a piece of paper to Fiona's attention. She received it, read its contents, and smiled.

'And to clarify your position, why did you arrive on Arran where your cousin was staying?'

'I was collecting my car at an airport office. On the wall was a screen which flashed up an advert to further my bird spotting hobby. The board highlighted Ardrossan with a connection to Arran and my mobile phone alerted me to the Golden Eagles there. That is why I went to Arran.'

'Thank you, Mr Berlotti. I have no further questions.'

As soon as his questioning was over, Daniel brought out his mobile phone and started to text.

'Miss France,' invited the sheriff.

Fiona stood up slowly. She looked across at Mr Berlotti.

'Have you your passport with you?'

Daniel put his phone in his pocket. He hesitated for a moment then recalled the question. Then realised it would confirm his journey from Africa. That was a good omen.

He took his passport from his jacket pocket and waved it at Fiona.

'May I see it?

Daniel passed the navy-blue document to the court official who brought it to Fiona. She opened it and ran through the pages. She stopped at the visa to Kenya.

'Indeed, you were in Kenya. I hope you enjoyed your time there. Did you?'

'Yes, I saw some wildlife in the safari parks and on the shores of Lake Victoria was a wonderful array of waders and smaller colourful birds.'

'You must have some wonderful pictures. Have you your camera in your possession?'

'Er..yes...but I was told not to have one in court.'

'I think we can wave that rule, for the time being. Can you show me some pictures of Nairobi?'

'Certainly, I have a few.' Daniel opened his camera and located the first picture of Nairobi he took when he landed. He handed the phone with a photo of the Nairobi market in riotous colour to Fiona, once more through the court official.

Fiona scrolled through his city snaps to the end. Then she returned to the first photo and scrolled backwards.

'Do you ever delete any photos?'

'I do that at the end of a holiday. I can reflect then what I keep and what I delete.'

'Seems you deleted all the Lake Victoria bird photos. Not a bird in sight.' Fiona looked at Daniel and in that moment's silence the jury must have wondered how a tourist could lose Lake Victoria pictures.

Daniel remained silent realising his mistake.

'I see you had a one-month visa to Kenya,' stated Fiona. 'But in fact, you only stayed three days. Bit of a waste of a visa, I'd say.'

Mr Sinclair stood up. He opened his mouth. Thought better then sat down.

'Do you know what you can buy almost over the counter in Kenya, Mr Berlotti?'

'Coffee?'

'Well of course but Kenya is the only country, after Thailand banned it, to sell Carbofuran legally.'

Daniel screwed up his eyes and looked accusingly at Fiona.

'I put it to you Mr Berlotti, your three days in Kenya was to obtain Carbofuran and come to Blackwaterfoot to murder your cousin.'

Daniel looked down. He was lost for words, and none came out of his mouth. Then one word did. 'Preposterous,' he said. But the lacuna said more than that one word.

The summing up was relatively brief as they had covered all the salient points.

Either Daniel was a bird spotter who accidentally bought Carbofuran instead of cocaine in Glasgow. His bird pictures never surfaced so his Kenyan bird observer break was in doubt. He was in Kenya where Carbofuran was used to kill lions. It was no longer a case of circumstantial evidence as Mr Sinclair suggested. But it was for the jury to decide whether Daniel's intentions were that of an innocent ornithologist tourist with a passion for cocaine, or as a murderer attempting to kill his cousin. The jury left the court at 12:45 p.m. with both options to consider. In their upstairs room of the court, lunch was brought to them. Then the doors were slammed shut. They had a working lunch with an agenda to consume.

Tony enjoyed lunch at the procurator fiscal's office, and he was questioned about the American system by Fiona's interested colleagues. They had just poured their second coffee when the telephone rang. The jury had reached their decision. The court would resume in half an hour.

As Tony walked over to the court with Fiona, Ruth Anderson joined them briefly.

'I do hope they come to an honest decision.'

'That's the system we have. The jury always hear the two sides of each case and bring their decision to the Sheriff,' said Fiona.

'May the Lord, be with us all.'

'Indeed,' said Fiona as they entered the court.

When all were in position, Sheriff Moffat lifted his eyes to the jury.

'Will the Jury Chair, be upstanding, please?'

A man going bald and wearing a sports jacket and grey trousers rose, holding a piece of paper.

'Has the jury reached a decision?'

'We have My Lord, a unanimous decision.'

The court official stepped forward to take the piece of paper and gave it to the Sheriff. He read it slowly while Daniel's eyes were upon him and hoping the verdict would go his way.

'Please stand Mr Berlotti,' the Sheriff said, and Daniel stood erect as a soldier on parade.

'The jury have found you guilty of being in possession of a dangerous substance, namely Carbofuran. Regarding the other matter, the jury also find you guilty of the attempted murder of Mr Tony Lupino.'

The silence remained as the case came to an end.

'I shall not require to seek avizandum as the punishment for these crimes are prescribed. Mr Berlotti for the possession of Carbofuran, you are sentenced to four years in prison. For the attempted murder of Tony Lupino, you shall serve twenty-one years. You will be detained for twenty-five years in total. I thank the jury for their work. The case is now concluded.'

'Court Rise,' shouted the court official and all stood up immediately, except Daniel, whose hands supported his fallen head. After a moment he sat up and mouthed what Fiona heard was 'Can I appeal?' but she knew the evidence had been overwhelming and such a course of action was ill advised. By the shaking of his head Mr Sinclair seemed to have reached the same conclusion.

Chapter 17: Back To Blackwaterfoot

Tony's trip back on the MV Caledonian Isles gave him some thinking time. He stood outside on the second deck as the wind blew his hair to one side and then the other. Clouds sped by overhead as if in a race. And the aroma from the boat's kitchen met his approval.

As a lawyer, he knew truth was paramount and important, but would the islanders see it from his point of view? Then his phone rang.

'Yes, good. What's the date to be?' Fine. I'll pick them up before I go. Brilliant. Yeah, thanks for all your help. G'bye.'

He switched off his mobile phone and by the time he had finalised what had to be done, passengers were starting to form a queue to leave the boat.

Once more at the wheel of his Ford Kuga he set off on the String Road to Blackwaterfoot and was soon in the car park of the Kinloch Hotel.

He entered the hotel and found Babs, Robbie's wife, at the reception desk.

'Hi Tony. How did the court case go,' she asked with a note of concern.

'Just perfect. Attempted murder and illegal possession, 25 years in total. And his behaviour just ain't good. He's not likely get any remission for being a good boy. Suits me, of course.'

'But attempted murder? Who was the intended victim?'

Tony stroked his chin. 'You know perhaps I should have one final get-together and lay all the demons down. Do you think that could be arranged?'

'Of course, I'll get on to that but Tony, who was the intended victim?'

Tony smiled. His eyelashes flashed up and down twice.

'You don't mean you were, do you?'

Tony nodded, smiled, and left for his room.

Tony had received an e-mail notification of his revised return ticket date to New York and had advised the NYPD of the date and time of his arrival in four days' time. He also telephoned the American Embassy to inform them of the court outcome and his intended date of return. That gave him forty-eight hours to prepare his statement to whoever might turn up at the hotel to hear him.

Unknown to Tony, the word had got out. Babs notified the Harbour Shop which put the advert with a gold border around the announcement in the front window. The factor that it was a free talk, and of course, from the fallen celebrity, ensured many were going to attend.

On the evening in question, Tony regaled himself once more in his Red Indian attire. He sported two charcoal finger-stroked on his cheeks and descended into the room at the appointed time of 8:30 pm. This time he was met mostly by smiles, but he was also aware many felt he had blotted his copybook.

Robbie, dressed in a tartan jacket and matching bow tie, introduced Tony once more.

'In all the years I have been the hotel manager here in Blackwaterfoot, I have never had a more interesting, puzzling, amazing, musician, cook, gold finder, body recovering, herbalist, aeroplane discoverer and from what I have heard and now seen in the Annan Banner, a clever court witness and American prosecutor.'

Most of the audience clapped.

'But I want to leave it to Tony to explain which parts are true and which are, well, not so true. He wants to come clean.'

'You mean lies?' asked a voice from the back of the hall.

'I did not say lies,' replied Robbie with a sharp look towards the back of the lounge.

Tony stood up and lightly patted Robbie arm. 'Maybe he is right. I'll certainly give evidence of me not telling the truth but were they devious lies or white lies which could be forgiven? I leave that for you to decide but hear me out is what I ask.'

Many heads nodded and some others went to the bar to top up their drinks to fuel any argument which might ensue.

'I dress as a Sioux chief....I am not. I can't deny I come from a Nu Yok Mafia family either, but I'm not of that ilk either.' Tony took off his headdress and then disappeared behind a screen. From there he stripped into a collar and tie with slacks. He folded the screen. He brought out the Indian attire.

'Robbie, a fancy party or a display at the reception, it is yours to use. I hope it provides some fun.'

Robbie gathered the traditional costume and laid it carefully behind the bar. 'That's a most generous gift Tony. I'm sure I'll find uses to wear it.'

From the back of the room, the same grumpy intruder spoke. 'And wear it in the bedroom. It will tickle Bab's fancy,' he laughed but there were too many tut tuts in opposition to his outburst.

'And my relationship with Alban Caskie? Well, he never existed.'

There was a sharp intake of breath from the gathered villagers. They were beginning to see Tony as a fraudster but no one yet, had said so.

'It would not be easy to arrive and be known instantly. I guess it was a need to be recognised and to be loved. Just to make an impact. Yes, I deceived you as I needed friends to talk to, real people. You see I prosecute Mafia cases in court. It makes many enemies doing that, especially as I was the son of a Godfather myself. I have police protection. They use unmarked cars to drive me to work and home again. No socialising. They moved me from one dwelling to another, often twice a month. I could never settle in any community. I was searching for that security, amidst new friendships. I can't explain it any other way. I was so relieved when the plane left JFK airport.'

'So, what about the gold? Was that stolen Mafia gold?'

'You know, yes it was. But I didn't find that out till recently, here on Arran. No, I brought that inherited gold to Arran to create some wealth for you. A bit of local excitement into the bargain.'

'It certainly was exciting,' said Eric taking his lager from his mouth as he spoke but leaving a frothy upper lip.

'I never gained a cent from it. But what I learned a few days ago was that the gold nuggets were stolen from Levi's Emporium in 1932 in Nu Yok. I have to return it. I've also clarified the gold's status with Edinburgh asking them to release the gems. You see, Levi's is still a Manhattan business, and they rightly want their gold nuggets returned. That's where they will be going. That's where they belong.'

Sympathetic understanding was etched on many faces. Then Babs spoke. 'Finding a WW II plane. I can't imagine you hid that one from us then discovered it.' There was open laughter at that remark.

Tony laughed. 'The problem is simple. I fell in love with Arran. Yes, probably the most remote part of Arran. It's a part not many see. But the weather had uncovered a wing and my curiosity found the plane. Now many thought it was my Sioux instinct which made the discovery. It just shows one lie leads to another. I pretended the spirit of the Sioux led me there. Yes, I was in a surreal world, I admit.'

Tony took a large sip of Irn Bru which he had brought to a nearby table. 'The saddest day was when Sergeant Murdoch asked me if I could help him find a missing teenager. I think he too, thought I had Sioux Indian powers of detection. But no. I have had many fatal accident enquiries at work and when the deceased are young, if not killed by guns or drugs, the so-called easy cases, they were likely to have drowned. The youth's fascination with water is a fact. It led me to the nearest loch in the area where I found Callum's clothes. Simple detection work gleaned from my professional cases and know-how, that's all it was.'

'That puts you in the good books for me,' said Ruth, who appeared from the fourth row of chairs.

'Glad to see you again, Ruth.'

Ruth smiled at Tony. 'Keep walking on straight paths, Mr Lupino.'

'Good advice, Ruth.'

'Not my advice. Hebrews Chapter 12 verse 13.'

'Ah of course,' said Tony.

Fortunately, a tea trolley appeared with coffees and tea and a host of delicacies from pancakes and scones to Angel cake and a chocolate log. Fingers approached.

'Well now my cousin is safely behind bars, there's no need for me to tell you about the court case. Friday's Arran Banner has a full report. The case is there for you all to read. That leaves just one final matter.'

But Tony's voice was lost in the movement of approaching hot drinks and side plates to support their sweet tooth. Babs lingered for a moment.

'You were saying there was just one other matter?'

'Yes, I'll leave that for you to tell the village.' Bab's tilted her head slightly, encouraging Tony to divulge his parting shot.

'You know Shore Cottage on the sea front?'

'Er...yes, the one for sale?'

'It's no longer Shore Cottage.'

'Really, I did not know that.'

Tony smiled a wicked smile. 'It's Tanna Cottage now.'

'Oh,' said Babs.

Tony put his hand in his pocket and pulled out a set of keys.

'Don't tell me you are moving to Blackwaterfoot?' asked Babs.

'I'll come each summer. But I'll retire in five years' time. By then I hope to have Scottish citizenship.'

Babs smiled. 'That would be great.'

'I'd need a couple of referees though,' Tony said with the look of a sheepish bloodhound.

'I think you have two already?' said Babs.

Tony smiled. He knew where his future lay.

The End

Your Extra Short Stories

Ruffled Feathers At Blackwaterfoot, as you will have noticed, is not too long a book. It is a classic novella size. So, I felt I should give readers a bonus. Welcome to my world of dreams, for that is where my books come from. Each dream is a short story for you to enjoy.

Authors are often asked how they can write so many books when most people have usually only one story to tell. This is my thirty-first book. I respond by saying I dream. I dream every night and remember most of them the following morning. I am one of 5% of the public who remember their dreams on waking.

I now give you a selection of twelve of my dreams; one is from a friend. Some of these dreams appear in the book *A Dream Net*. This book was compiled by no fewer than twenty-one contributors from as far afield as Siberia and Kyrgyzstan and as local as Eire and The United Kingdom. The entire royalties of this book are donated to the Alzheimer Society and those who wish to support this charity, should purchase this fascinating £10 book, which will soon be published. To set the dreams in context, I have explained the dream processes and some facts about dreams, which I trust you will find interesting.

Dreams most likely happen during Rapid Eye Movement sleep. There are five phases of sleep in a sleep cycle:

Stage 1: Light sleep, slow eye movement, and reduced muscle activity. This stage forms 4 to 5 percent of total sleep.

Stage 2: Eye movement stops, and brain waves become slower, with occasional bursts of rapid waves called sleep spindles. This stage forms forty-five to fify-five percent of total sleep.

Stage 3: Extremely slow brain waves called delta waves begin to appear, interspersed with smaller, faster waves. This accounts for 4 to 6 percent of total sleep.

Stage 4: The brain produces delta waves almost exclusively. It is difficult to wake someone during stages 3 and 4, which together are called 'deep sleep'. There is no eye movement or muscle activity. People awakened while in deep sleep do not adjust immediately and often feel disoriented for several minutes after waking up.

Stage 5: This stage is known as rapid eye movement (REM). Breathing becomes more rapid, irregular, and shallow, eyes jerk rapidly in various directions, and limb muscles become temporarily paralyzed. Heart rate increases, blood pressure rises, and males develop penile erections. When people awaken during REM sleep, they often describe bizarre and illogical tales. These are dreams. Neuroscience offers explanations linked to the rapid eye movement (REM) phase of sleep as a likely candidate for the cause of dreams.

What Are Dreams?

Dreams are a universal human experience that can be described as a state of consciousness characterized by sensory, cognitive, and emotional occurrences during sleep. Reports of dreams are full of emotional and vivid experiences that contain themes, concerns, dream figures, and objects that correspond closely to waking life.

Nightmares

Nightmares are distressing dreams that cause the dreamer to feel a number of disturbing emotions. Common reactions to a nightmare include fear and anxiety. They can occur in both adults and children, and causes include:

- Stress
- Fear
- Trauma
- Emotional difficulties
- Illness
- Use of certain medications or drugs

Lucid Dreams

Lucid dreaming is the dreamer who is aware that they are dreaming. They may have some control over their dream. This measure of control can vary between lucid dreams. They often occur in the middle of a regular dream when the sleeping person realizes suddenly that they are dreaming.

Some people experience lucid dreaming at random, while others have reported being able to increase their capacity to control their dreams.

Interpretations

What goes through our minds just before we fall asleep could affect the content of our dreams. For example, during exam time, students may dream about course content. People in a relationship may dream of their partner. Web developers may see programming codes.

These circumstantial observations suggest that elements from the everyday re-emerge in dream-like imagery during the transition from wakefulness to sleep.

Characters

Studies have examined the "characters" that appear in dream reports and how they, the dreamers, identify them. A study of characters found:

- Forty-eight percent of characters represented a named person known to the dreamer
- Thirty-five percent of characters were identified by their social role (for example, policeman) or relationship to dreamer (such as a friend)
- Sixteen percent were not recognized

Among named characters:

- Thirty-two percent were identified by appearance
- Twenty-one percent were identified by behaviour
- Forty-five percent were identified by face
- Forty-four percent were identified by 'just knowing'

Affection and joy were commonly associated with known characters and were used to identify them even when these emotional attributes were inconsistent with those of the waking state.

Memories

The concept of 'repression' dates back to Freud. Freud maintained that undesirable memories could become suppressed in the mind. Dreams ease repression by allowing these memories to be reinstated.

A study showed that sleep does not help people forget unwanted memories. Instead, REM sleep might even counteract the voluntary suppression of memories, making them more accessible for retrieval.

There are two types of temporal effects which characterize the incorporation of memories into dreams.

Dream-Lag

Dream-Lag is when the images, experiences, or people that emerge in dreams are images, experiences, or people you have seen recently, perhaps the previous day or a week before.

The idea is that certain types of experiences take a week to become encoded into long-term memory, and some of the images from the consolidation process will appear in a dream.

Memory Types And Dreaming

Two types of memory can form the basis of a dream.

These are:

- Autobiographical memories, or long-lasting memories about the self
- Episodic memories, which are memories about specific episodes or events

Researchers suggest that memories of personal experiences are experienced fragmentarily and selectively during dreaming. The purpose may be to integrate these memories into the long-lasting autobiographical memory.

A hypothesis stating that dreams reflect waking-life experiences is supported by studies investigating the dreams of psychiatric patients and patients with sleep disorders. In short, their daytime symptoms and problems are reflected in their dreams.

One paper hypothesises that the main aspect of traumatic dreams is to communicate an experience that the dreamer has in the dream but does not understand. This can help an individual reconstruct and come to terms with past trauma. Some themes are familiar to many people, such as flying, falling, and arriving late. The 55 themes identified are:

- School, teachers, and studying

- Being chased or pursued
- Sexual experiences
- Falling
- Arriving too late
- A living person being dead
- A person now dead being alive
- Flying or soaring through the air
- Failing an examination
- Being on the verge of falling
- Being frozen with fright
- Being physically attacked
- Being nude
- Eating delicious food
- Swimming
- Being locked up
- Insects or spiders
- Being killed
- Losing teeth
- Being tied up, restrained, or unable to move
- Being inappropriately dressed
- Being a child again
- Trying to complete a task successfully
- Being unable to find a toilet,
- Discovering a new room at home
- Having superior knowledge or mental ability
- Losing control of a vehicle
- Fire
- Wild, violent beasts
- Seeing a face very close to you
- Snakes

- Having magical powers
- Vividly sensing, but not necessarily seeing or hearing, a presence in the room
- Finding money
- Floods or tidal waves
- Killing someone
- Seeing yourself as dead
- Being half-awake and paralyzed in bed
- People behaving in a menacing way
- Seeing yourself in a mirror
- Being a member of the opposite sex
- Being smothered, unable to breathe
- Encountering God in some form
- Seeing a flying object crash
- Earthquakes
- Seeing an angel
- Part animal, part human creatures
- Tornadoes or strong winds
- Being at the movie
- Seeing extra-terrestrials
- Travelling to another planet
- Being an animal
- Seeing a UFO
- Someone having an abortion
- Being an object

Some dream themes appear to change over time. What do they mean?

Relationships: Some have hypothesized that one cluster of typical dreams, including being an object in danger, falling, or being chased, is related to interpersonal conflicts.

Sexual concepts: Another cluster that includes flying, sexual experiences, finding money, and eating delicious food is associated with libidinal and sexual motivations.

Fear of embarrassment: A third group, containing dreams that involve being nude, failing an examination, arriving too late, losing teeth, and being inappropriately dressed, is associated with social concerns and a fear of embarrassment.

Music In Dreams

Music in dreams is rarely studied in scientific literature. However, in a study of thirty-five professional musicians and thirty non-musicians, the musicians experienced twice as many dreams featuring music, when compared with non-musicians. Musical dream frequency was related to the age of commencement of musical instruction but not to the daily load of musical activity. Nearly half of the recalled music was non-standard, suggesting that original music can be created in dreams.

Left And Right Side Of The Brain

The right and left hemispheres of the brain seem to contribute in different ways to a dream formation. Researchers of one study concluded that the left hemisphere seems to provide dream origin while the right hemisphere provides dream vividness, figurativeness, and affective activation levels.

A study of adolescents aged ten to seventeen years found that those who were left-handed were more likely to experience lucid dreams and to remember dreams within other dreams.

Forgetting Dreams

Studies of brain activity suggest that most people over the age of ten years dream between four and six times each night, but many people rarely remember dreaming.

It is often said that five minutes after a dream, people have forgotten fifty percent of its content, increasing to ninety percent another five minutes later.

Most dreams are entirely forgotten by the time someone wakes up, but it is not known precisely why dreams are so hard to remember. Steps that may help improve dream recall include:

- Waking up naturally and not with an alarm
- Focusing on the dream as much as possible upon waking
- Writing down as much about the dream as possible upon waking
- Making recording dreams a routine

Who Remembers Their Dreams?

There are factors that can potentially influence who remembers their dreams, how much of the dream remains intact, and how vivid it is:

Age: Over time, a person is likely to experience changes in sleep timing, structure, and electroencephalographic (EEG) activity.

Evidence suggests that dream recall progressively decreases from the beginning of adulthood, but not in older age. Dreams also become less intense. This evolution occurs faster in men than women, with gender differences in the content of dreams.

Gender: A study of dreams experienced by 108 males and 110 females found no differences between the amount of aggression, friendliness, sexuality, male characters, weapons, or clothes that feature in the content.

Sleep disorders: Dream recall is heightened in patients with insomnia, and their dreams reflect the stress associated with their condition. The dreams of people with narcolepsy may be more negative.

Who Dreams?

Children's dreams

A study investigating anxiety dreams in 103 children aged nine to eleven years found:

Females more often had dreams containing anxiety than males, although they could not remember their dreams as often.

Girls dreamt more often than boys about the loss of another person, falling, socially disturbing situations, small or aggressive animals, family members, and other female people they may or may not recognize.

Bereavement

It is widely believed that oppressive dreams are frequent in people going through a time of bereavement. A study analysing dream quality, as well as the linking of oppressive dreams in bereavement, discovered that oppressive dreams:

- Were more frequent in the first year of bereavement
- Were more likely in those experiencing symptoms of anxiety and depression

In another study of 278 people experiencing bereavement:

- Fifty-eight percent reported dreams of their deceased loved ones, with varying levels of frequency
- Most participants had dreams that were either pleasant or both pleasant and disturbing, and few reported purely disturbing dreams

- Prevalent themes included pleasant past memories or experiences, the deceased being free of illness, memories of the deceased's illness or time of death, the deceased in the afterlife appearing comfortable and at peace, and the deceased person communicating a message
- Sixty percent felt that their dreams impacted upon their bereavement process

Does everyone dream in colour?

Researchers discovered in a study that:

- About 80 percent of participants younger than 30 years old dreamed in colour
- At 60 years old, 20 percent said they dreamed in colour

Researchers speculated that colour television might play a role in the generational difference. Older people reported that both their colour dreams and black and white dreams were equally vivid. However, younger participants said that their black and white dreams were of poorer quality.

Can dreams predict the future?

Some dreams may seem to predict future events. Some researchers claim that this is possible, but there is not enough evidence to prove it (read 9/11 by Catherine Czerkawska, the penultimate story of this book). Most often, this seems to be due to coincidence, a false memory, or the unconscious mind connecting together known information.

Dreams may help people learn more about their feelings, beliefs, and values. Images and symbols that appear in dreams will have meanings and connections that are specific to each person. People looking to make sense of their dreams should think about what each part of the dreams mean to them as an individual.

Now follows my own dreams. I hope you enjoy the stories although you might find some surreal, some amusing and some bizarre. Good night. Sleep well. Don't let the bed bugs bite. And above all sound sleep and sweet repose. Sleep on your back so you don't squash your nose...and the dreams will flow.

Dream One: The Glasgow Bus

(The first two dreams featuring Arran)

Glasgow awoke from its usual dowdy, cloudy drizzle to shed sunshine all over the green city that afternoon. I had been visiting my blind cousin Brian who lives near the Great Western Road, in the city and whose memory is amazingly accurate. He can tell which car I have had in the past in ordered sequence and he enquires if the latest has had its first service. Blind since birth, he lives in an imaginary universe of mechanics and a solid family awareness.

I lived in Glasgow many years ago but was now living in Blackwaterfoot on the beautiful island of Arran, in my mind. I was heading home. I had in my satchel a novel, *A Lingering Crime*, and I had also purchased an Evening Times should the train journey south to Ardrossan require a crossword to fill.

From boarding a subway at Kelvinbridge station, I alighted at Buchanan Street station and then crossed over to Renfield Street and onward to the Central Station. I was in good time. I was not in a hurry. Pedestrians passed by at a good rate on their purposeful errands.

Yellow and green, the colours of Glasgow transport had their buses plying down Renfield Street's one-way lanes. I was aware of a bus slowing down and indeed it stopped just ahead of me. I think three passengers alighted. A man around forty years of age with a thread of a black beard around his chin walked back up the street; an older woman with a head of blue-rinsed hair and a warm royal blue scarf took her time to leave the bus and finally a younger woman carrying two bags. I caught a glimpse of her child behind her. The bus's doors closed and the 38 bus to Rouken Glen resumed its journey.

That was when, by instinct, I darted into the road chasing the bus. The child was suspended by a harness trapped by the closed doors. I banged on the bus's side window as I approached the child. The driver caught my eye and waved me away. He did not stop for passengers once the doors were closed and he had obviously not seen the child, nor heard its whimpers. I grabbed the dangling child and unclipped the safety clasp on her back. Instantly she broke loose into my arms as the bus continued on its way, with the trapped harness flapping like a streamer on a summer's day-outing. My last sight of the bus was to see passengers on the near side with mouths open, remonstrating to the driver to stop but I knew I had saved that child from dreadful injury.

Then unexpectedly as the bus was slowing down, I looked behind to see and hear the child's worried mother approach at pace, shouting hysterically. I felt a solid bang on the back of my head. I glimpsed for a second at the offending white van's wing mirror before I hit the ground. I held the child close to me in a firm embrace and fell on my back hitting my head against the road surface.

I think I was in the Glasgow Royal Infirmary for two weeks, it may have been longer. I had grown an untidy beard for sure and recalled my grandmother had been the matron of this hospital more than a century ago. A doctor was at the foot of my bed. He was obviously pleased to see I had recovered despite a heavy white bandage, wrapped around my head.

'Can I go home now?'

'Do you know why you have been in hospital?' he asked in a concerned manner.

'No,' I replied.

The doctor opened a newspaper which he held. He read to me. It seemed I had saved a child from death and her mother seeing me on the road unconscious, had contacted the press after the ambulance and police. The papers jumped at the story and began a campaign for me to be given an award.

Instantly I found myself at Buckingham Palace. The room was large, and many seats were regimentally set out. When my name was called I stepped forward. Prince Charles decorated me with some medal and, as it was pinned to my chest, I woke up. The pin seemed to have gone through my pyjamas and pained me. The dream was over. It was approaching 7:15 am. At breakfast time I told my wife about this dream.

I then sat down to remember many of my other vivid dreams which I have dreamt. I thought dreams might make an interesting book and so I asked some friends if they remembered their dreams. I asked if they could send them to me. The responses I got from all over the world were overwhelming, and wonderful as you are about to discover. But first, it's time to meet my parrot, Kofi, for the first of my two parrot dreams. Yet again, this dream was set on Arran.

Dream 2: The Precocious Parrot

The head teacher of Shiskine primary school, near Blackwaterfoot, on the island of Arran had invited me to speak to the children, bringing with me my African Grey parrot, Kofi, in this dream. I had actually owned the bird for a number of years in Ghana, West Africa, when I worked there. It had been my constant partner, before I was married.

The children were thrilled to see and hear the parrot answer many of my mundane questions. I encouraged them to come up and stroke the parrot's head but not its red tail feather as that was a sensitive spot. The last child to come up was a boy. I think I called him Bobby in my dream. I can't be sure. However, as he lingered, I decided he could have Kofi perch on his arm. Clearly

Bobby loved Kofi and he was pleased to have been chosen to hold the parrot. He spoke to it and the parrot inclined his head. It understood his questions and replied appropriately. The class laughed as Bobby continued to ask the parrot questions until the mid-day bell rang. The children all stood up ready to play in the playground. But I had to apologise. It was not break time at all. The bell sound emanated from Kofi's beak. The class were in hoots of laughter. Five minutes later it was the real school bell and Kofi repeated its tone as soon as the janitor had stopped ringing his clanger.

I was invited into the staff room at morning break time, where Kofi fascinated the teachers, twiddling a ginger nut biscuit like a card trickster in his claw. They sat drinking their Guatemalan coffee. I was given tea, my preference.

Then all hell broke loose. It began with a voice approaching the staff room, it was an angry mother. Her fist knocked on the staff door making the frosted glass rattle. I thought she might break it.

The head teacher went to open the door and I saw her take a deep breath in preparation for confrontation. She placed her hand on the handle as the door burst open. The woman continued to raise her voice in anger, as she advanced. It seemed Bobby, her son, had phoned his mother at break-time and told her he had held a parrot in class. Straight away she made her way to confront the head teacher, in her Paisley-patterned apron with her curlers still in place. The gist of her anger was that Bobby suffered allergies, particularly of feathers. His bed cushion was full of polystyrene marble-sized balls and not a feather ever entered their home. The woman accused the head teacher of not recalling Bobby's medical notes. No Feathers. That bird had bloody f e a t h e r s, she spelled out. That bird had been very close to Bobby's face. Through sobbing tears, the mother informed the open-mouthed staff, that she was taking Bobby to the doctor, right there and then. She did not want to suffer another restless night with a child gasping for breath.

The atmosphere was tense in the staff room. Kofi sensed the atmosphere and said, 'Oh dear.' I finished my tea and left the head and her staff to cry and comfort one another.

The next scene was to find a bouquet of flowers at my front door. There was no label on them, and I had no idea who the kind person was who left them. Later that afternoon the front doorbell rang. I opened the door to find an attractive woman in a summer dress with immaculate auburn wavy hair. I did not recognise her, but I did recognise Bobby who stood beside her.

She told me she had sent the flowers as a peace offering. Apparently when the doctor sent the boy to the allergy expert at the hospital, they found Bobby was no longer allergic to feathers. It was a doze of Kofi, my African parrot, which had been the answer. His feathers acted as a biological immunotherapy on Bobby and so his feather allergy was totally cured. She could not have been more excited or happy. I was pleased for her.

I got out of bed at 8:05 am feeling very satisfied at the outcome, no matter how improbable it might have been.

Dream 3: The Missing Parrot

It was after I stubbed my finger on a stubborn doorbell, this dream took place. Earlier in the day, I had found myself in A&E being attended for a mallet finger. My middle finger now wore a splint. As a consequence, my erect middle finger was offensive if I held it up to the world. It was uncomfortable at times in bed but did not stop this dream.

I found myself returning home after my hospital visit that day with an extra splint given to me when I told the nurse about my amazing parrot. She told me these splints were indestructible and so it would be an ideal present and certainly of interest to Kofi. But when I returned home, my dream was underway. I found the lounge door open and Kofi's cage open. I raced upstairs and checked all rooms. He was often in the bathroom watching me shave in the morning, but he was not there. I called his name out, but there was no reply. I returned downstairs with an audible heartbeat. Then I broke into a sweat in seeing the conservatory door ajar and I realised with dread, that Kofi had joined his friends in the sky.

I ran about the garden and called his name while looking for any swaying branches. But it seemed he had taken an inquisitive flight far beyond the sanctuary of his cage, our garden, our town perhaps? I phoned the police to report a missing parrot. I was told a parrot had been seen in the grounds of the local hospital. It must have come to the hospital to look for me, of course. I drove out to the hospital there and then, speeding around 100 mph to get there quickly. The car's tyres squeaked and screeched as I took tight corners. I drove through red traffic lights. Fortunately, the traffic cops were nowhere to be seen.

I walked round the hospital grounds calling 'Kofi, Kofi' to the branches. There were many more trees by the mental health wards. I ventured near them and again called my pet's name. A young man came out of the hospital and approached me. 'You looking for coffee?'

'Yes,' I said with a smile as the light was fading. 'Kofi, where are you?'

'Come with me. I could do with a warm cup of coffee too,' the man said. I was having no luck finding my missing bird and I knew, as it was quite dark, Kofi would be roosting on a branch somewhere.

I accepted the man's invitation for coffee in the ward office as he sorted his papers. Then he telephoned a doctor. 'Can you section him? Well, he's been speaking to trees and asking them for coffee.'

I struggled to break free but two men in white coats arrived and took me into a ward where pyjamas were neatly laid at the end of a bed. I was instructed to get in them because it would be an early start I'd need, to find Kofi in the branches the following day. I relaxed in bed feeling they were doing me a good turn after all. But when I woke early the following morning it was a different shift and a large rotund nurse saw me dress. 'Where are you going, mate?' he growled at me. I told him I was ready to resume my search of Kofi in the trees.

'Oh no you are not. You wait for Dr Ffrench-Blake's morning round before you are going anywhere.'

'But I'm not a patient. I'm not mentally ill,' I protested.

'That's what they all say in here. Now get back into bed and await the doctor.' His command was so strong I could not refuse. I looked at my fellow bed companions. Many had no teeth only gums. 'You'll get coffee later in the day,' shouted one and all heads nodded their agreement. I took that as a sign of support from the patients. Daylight came to me when curtains were pulled back. Dr Ffrench-Blake the psychiatrist was doing his ward round. Grateful patients swallowed the green liquid medication or the handful of pills on offer. Eventually the doctor arrived at my bed and looked through his notes. He looked confused. I told him I was looking for my lost parrot and by mistake I found myself in a mental hospital. 'I am really not ill', I told him.

'And neither you are,' he replied. 'I heard about your missing parrot on the 7 am local news this morning. I hope you find your parrot soon. What was its name?'

'Kofi, it is,' I informed him.

He smiled at me and nodded his head.

'Too early for coffee,' shouted a bed mate. But the psychiatrist's diagnoses did the trick.

I left the mental hospital and returned home dejected. I opened the door and saw to my amazement Kofi climbing his metal pole to his open cage. I relaxed.

I awoke.

Dream 4: A Game of Football

I found myself dreaming of playing football. My brother was in the team. I was the goalkeeper, saving crosses, shots and prospective high punts. The goalie, of course, is the last line of defence. I came with the ball to the edge of the penalty area and threw the ball to my brother, Bruce. He was on the wing and like a dancing nymph he wove his way goal wards. The other goalkeeper advanced and as he was a few feet away, Bruce chipped the ball over him, and the ball trickled into the empty net. It was the only goal of the game. I ran to celebrate his goal at the halfway line and gave him a strong cuddle. I could not let him go. I held on to him until I woke.

My younger brother, Bruce, died four years before this dream.

Dream 5: Mother's Dream

I am reminded of an incident in 1968 when I lived with my family in Glasgow. It was not my dream but my mother's. She had a vivid dream that previous night and she told my older sister the following morning, to make our own family meal without her, at the end of the day. She had to travel.

I remember that evening meal. It was cod in a white parsley sauce, with mashed potato and carrots. My sister, Joan, made the meal and it was eaten in silence as we tried to come to terms with our mother's sudden disappearance. My mother's mother, my grandmother, was in a care home in Ayrshire, Haley House, on the periphery of Largs. We loved to visit her, and I'd look out of her room's window and see the Isle of Cumbrae. We sometimes took Gran to Nardini's Cafe where we scoffed their wonderful ice cream or Knickerbockers'

Glory. Those were happy outings. I wondered if my mother had gone to Largs.

Later that night mother returned with a calm, untroubled look on her face. She informed us that she had to visit her mother that day. She arrived and went to her room. Gran smiled at her only child. They spoke little but Mum held her hand and Gran closed her eyes, never to open them.

She explained her sudden departure quite simply. She had heard her mother call her in a dream the previous night and she knew she had to visit her the very next morning.

Dream 6: The Fishing Net

It was from Fraserburgh's Harbour that the fishing boat left on the early summer's evening. I recall that fateful summer holiday which snuffed out the life of my stillborn sister. Sadness and bewilderment was layered on my mind. Boarding the fishing boat was escapism for me. I was the lone landlubber on the fishing boat – no minister was ever allowed onboard for superstitious reasons beyond my ken and so the fishing trip I was promised, was without parental attendance.

The dream started with a memorable mug of tea, drowned with condensed milk. Consequently, it was served sweet but helped me to cope with the swaying motions of the vessel. It was nearing the third hour as the boat was heading for Lybster on the extreme north-northeast coast of Scotland when light faded and the work of harvesting the sea began.

I was given a line with no bait. The green nylon line had sixteen hooks shaded by various colours of plastic strips. I did as I was instructed and stood at the edge of the boat having slipped my hooks overboard and let them drop to the seabed. As soon as I raised the line, I felt tugs. Mackerel had attached themselves to the hooks in great numbers. I struggled to bring some of them aboard.

Before any fisherman saw my difficulties and came to assist me, the mackerel, as if directed by a company major, turned away from the boat and I followed on, diving headlong into the choppy water. I had no time to shout, and the boast's engine must have drowned the shock I expressed as I entered the cold water. I felt a peaceful descent into the dark sea and realised after a few moments that I must have drowned. I floated and swam like a fish until a dolphin nudged me. It swam alongside me, and I took hold of its dorsal fin. I kept my feet together, streamlining the dolphin's progress. It brought me to the seabed after a while and to a crevice in the rocks. It was about my bedtime, so I slept secure in the knowledge that the dolphin had become my guard and hovered around until the day broke.

It seemed a short sleep, but I could see the light of the sea surface above me when I woke. However, there was much to see on the seabed. A submarine lay quite nearby. I approached it. It had U507 on its turret. A WW II victim.

The German submarine, still rusting while sunk in the sandy ground at such an angle it seemed to be giving a Nazi salute, seemed interesting. I swam over to it and amid sharp eroding metal, I entered. I was not the first to do so. Many small fish were already in the submarine, making it a sanctuary from larger fish. They tickled me. There were no bodies to encounter, just bones. But an Enigma secret communication lay battered. A last-minute attempt at destroying the German secret coding which unknown to them at the time was already in the hands of decoders at Bletchley Park lay before me. I left the submarine as it seemed too eerie for me.

Then a large squid approached with dancing tentacles. They wound round me like a Boa Constrictor snake. I gasped as the tentacles tightened around my body. Then a white shark swam close by and decided the squid was its meal. It attacked two of its tentacles and suddenly I was released as the squid fought for its survival. I patted the white shark on its back as I swum past.

I met King Neptune who was enthroned on his seaweed draped throne. His green clad regal chair was a boulder cut out to seat him and he held his trident before me. He asked me what I was doing, and I told him, that I must have drowned. I had been on a fishing boat and fell over. He told me I was one of many fishermen who had drowned. He descended his throne and in a cave behind him, he invited me to enter.

There were many who turned their heads and smiled inanely. As they greeted me, I detected Cornish, Aberdonian, Yorkshire and Lancashire accents of smiling fishermen. I also detected the Hanseatic accents of north German sailors drinking beer with British sailors. No longer enemies of the mid-century world conflict, they shared jokes. There were no arms or ammunition in sight, but fraternal gestures abounded. I waved at them; they waved silently at me, then I turned around. King Neptune had gone, and I swam away, with a wave to the drowned former foes, towards the light of daytime on land. As I broke the surface, I realised I was near the shore. A few rocks lined the shoreline, and I swam to them. I climbed up one rugged boulder and took more gasps of fresh air. I awoke.

Dream 7: Boxing Day 2006

It was Christmas and I was disturbed. I felt uncomfortable as I slept in bed. I got up twice in a dozed state and returned to bed. My wife asked if I was okay, and I grunted my response. I had been sleepwalking. But before I awoke on Christmas Day, I had dreamt that the house shook. I was sure the pictures on the walls were hanging at rakish angles, that the dining room table was on its side and the dog was trapped underneath it. The bed came crashing through from the first floor to the kitchen below and windows cracked and broke, shedding splinters of glass around the house. The dog's paws were bleeding, but she licked out the shards and would not let me touch her.

My wife kissed me wishing me a Merry Christmas and I responded with my assertion that an earthquake had hit us in Dumfries. It was not the traffic noise of a lorry accident nearby but a real earthquake, I was sure of it. I knew I had been dreaming. But I did recall my recollections so well. I repeated them to my wife later that Christmas morning.

Around 10.30 am on Boxing Day I set off with our collie for his morning walk. I walked down the cycle path on a firm tar macadam surface with houses on either side of me. I expected I might hear the shouts of excited children playing with the presents Santa left the previous day. However, the screams were from adults as well. It seemed everyone was programmed to shout out simultaneously and I felt it a very surreal moment. Our collie dog was unsure too. He looked up at me several times, distracted from the scents which always preoccupied his elongated snout.

Twenty minutes later I returned home. I opened the door, and my wife came to greet me with a worried look. That was an earthquake she informed me. Strangely, there was no experience of an earthquake on my dog walk but in houses all over Dumfries people had experienced an earthquake measuring 3.7 on the Richter scale on Boxing Day 2006 at 10.40 am. Not a spectacularly high rate on the world Richter scale but one of the UK's highest.

A little over a year before, on October 8th, 2005, an earthquake measuring 7.7 on the Richter scale erupted killing 75 thousand people and making as many homeless and injured. In reality, two months later in January 2006, I would find myself in the NWFP of the Islamic Republic of Pakistan as the camp manager of 24,500 homeless and injured people at Mansehra.

Sadly, that crisis in Pakistan was not a dream. But my Christmas Morning 2006 dream predicted an earthquake 24 hours before it happened. Our British earthquakes are usually minimal. However, the movement of pictures on house walls must be signs of the earth's weak stability, or some force beyond our ken. Such dreams and resultant predictions are therefore not so unusual.

Dream 8: Ninety-Nine Lashings

This dream came to me while awaiting the final few entries for this book. I have worked in Pakistan and been to Oman, but this dream came to me from Iran, where I have never set foot. It is a frightening dream.

I was arrested in the hotel room by the Iranian police on a false charge of rape. I denied any knowledge of this offence. Nevertheless, I appeared in court the next day to formally deny the allegation.

At court I was given no legal representative, so I chose to defend myself. The alleged victim was first to give her account. I deceived her immediately.

'I am the defence lawyer. Have we ever met?'

'No sir.'

'I am European. Do you not recognise me?

'No sir, we have never met.'

'Exhibit A on the table is written in your hand is it not?

She looked at her statement. 'Yes, I wrote it.'

'It is an account of your rape is it not?'

'Yes, it is.'

'Where was this statement taken?

'At my house.'

'Did you request the police to visit you at your home?

'They always do.'

'I don't understand what you are saying?'

'This is the third time they have come to my home. I have given three statements, so far.'

'Are they all rape allegations?

'Yes.'

'May I ask how often have you been raped?'

'I've never been raped.'

'Are any of the police officers who interviewed you in court today?'

'Yes, Mr Malik.'

'Can you point to him?'

She does so.

'Thank you. You may sit down. I call upon Mr Malik.'

'Mr Malik you attended the home of the victim. Who sent you to her home?

'I don't know.'

'It's not a hard question. Presumably you were at your police station or in your police car and you were instructed to return to this lady's home. Who gave the order?'

Mr Malik took his time to answer but it was well worth the wait. 'The order came from the secret police.'

'And have the secret police asked you before to obtain a statement from the victim?'

'Yes, three times.'

'And was each occasion a rape allegation?'

Mr Malik was crunching his cap as he struggled with his answer.

'I remind you that you swore an oath to Allah, Peace be upon him, was each occasion a rape allegation?'

'Yes, each was a rape.'

'Thank you, Mr Malik. You may stand down.'

'And my dear Judges, that is the case. Indeed, there is no case. There is no evidence linking me to any rape. I further contend there was no rape of anyone.'

I sat down as the three judges met in a huddle.

Then the chair of the judges spoke. He avoided eye contact with me. 'We have come to our conclusion. By a majority, we find you guilty of rape. On Friday after prayers, you will be taken to Baharestan Square in Tehran where you will receive ninety-nine lashings with a judicial whip.'

'So, the Judiciary are under the command of the special police too. There is no evidence in this case,' I protested.

'Take him away.'

I counted the days down. They came very fast. On the dreaded Friday a car came to the police station, and I was bundled into it. It took me back to my hotel room where I was asked to change back into my usual clothing, and I had to have my passport returned from the front desk. I took out my wallet to pay for my stay, but they said they were in a hurry and not to pay. I said if I don't pay the police will find another charge against me, so they let me pay. The car took me to the Tehran airport. I asked what was happening. Apparently, I was never going to be given ninety-nine lashings. I was made an example of being one too many white businessmen in the country and some of them must have been spies, according to the secret police. They wanted to frighten me, which was all this dream was about. We shook hands and I boarded a flight to London, promising never to tell anyone what had happened. My lips are tightly sealed. I will not recall this story.

I awoke in a sweat.

Dream 9: The Vegetable Prize

This dream occurred in mid-winter 2020. The ground was as hard as iron, water like a stone. Yet my dream was a summer one, the warmth coming from the covers I clutched deep in sleep.

I was in an allotment. I'm not sure where but a row of terraced houses framed the growing area. I was not alone but other gardeners never raised their heads, and no verbal interaction took place.

Amid the growing tomatoes, the rich green spinach, rows of regimented onions and the wayward wafting of green beans on their cane supports, was my pride of joy. It lay on a light bed of straw and its skin was as smooth as a baby's bottom. It shone in its cradle as I took out a measuring tape. Three feet, four inches in length it measured, with a girth of twenty-three inches. To me it was a perfect specimen of a fully grown vegetable marrow, an outgrown courgette.

It must have been Thursday because early on the Saturday morning, two days later, I returned to the allotment with a sharp knife. I knelt down and cut it neatly at its neck. I lifted it and placed it carefully in the linen bag I had brought for the occasion.

I took it home and washed it till all the small particles of detritus on its cover fell off and I polished it like a cricket bowler's ball. Three hours later I was at the Community Hall where tables were laid out and a chalk board listed the prizes and the donors. Many donors seemed to have died and left amounts of money to ensure a good selection of fruit and vegetables competed at show each summer.

I was asked to display my marrow on a table marked 'Biggest on show'. That seemed appropriate. Before the judging got seriously underway and serious were the well-tanned gardening experts, a man entered the hall with what seemed like a hockey bag. It was long and when it was unzipped, he brought out an ill looking marrow. I was relieved such the yellow/brown pocked specimen did not match my bottle-green marrow. But his vegetable was put alongside mine. I screwed up my eyes. The lengths were about the same perhaps but the quality of mine would shine through. I was convinced.

Forty minutes later, the judges, all three of them, arrived at our table. My excitement grew. The prize was £25 and that would go a long way towards an evening meal with my wife that night. An inch tape was produced, and the lengths recorded. The girths were measured too. And re-checked, quite unnecessarily, I felt. I easily won that element, surely? The judges nodded to one another. Then the chief judge gave her result. The winner for the longest length marrow, by a winning margin of only one quarter of an inch, goes to Mr Alan Nicolson. I froze. How could this have happened? Surely a quarter of in inch did not matter when the specimens could not have been more different.

Mr Nicholson stepped forward and received his £25 and I applauded politely, without much enthusiasm at his good fortune and to show I was the contrite beaten finalist.

I lingered on to see other prizes being won. The best bunch of Tom Thumb tomatoes took the Margaret Bell trophy. The strangest looking carrot gained the Thomas Sidebotham prize; the most luscious leaves of a lettuce; The Daisy Althrop Cup and the length and freshness of stringer beans; the Connor McGrory prize. Each winner proudly came forward to collect their winning envelope. The event was coming to an end, and a few had already left the hall.

Then the Chief Judge made an announcement. 'And finally, we come to the Best on Show. We have had an eye on all that have appeared this afternoon, both fruit and vegetables. Many have been a delight to see, and much appreciation goes to the busy gardeners who have braved the elements to tend their crops. I can now announce that the winner of the Miss Massie Martin Prize for Best on Show and with the title of goes a cheque for £100....goes to....'

I felt TV was responsible for this elongated pause before any winner was announced. It seemed so inappropriate for a fruit or vegetable contest. Quite unnecessary.

'.... goes to Mr....Miller Caldwell for his gigantic marrow.'

A broad smile widened my face and I stepped forward. I shook the Judges' hands and received not only my envelope but the Best on Show Cup. It reminded me of the FA winners' cup, so I held it aloft.

'And will you be cooking the marrow tonight, may I ask?' asked the judge.

'It's too big a marrow for the two of us,' I replied.

It was then I recognised a lady in the hall. She was clearly on her day off. Nevertheless, I felt she should have it.

'As I said it would be too large a meal for us but perhaps the Apple Blossom Care Home should have it. Perhaps Mrs Pearson, if I give it to you, as Matron, you can take it to the chef at the Care Home and see what he can cook and do with it.'

Mrs Pearson came forward with a confident grin and received the vegetable with grateful thanks. I gave her the bag in which I had brought it, and I saw her struggle to hold it.

On the way home, I opened the envelope and saw the cheque for £100. I took my mobile phone out of my pocket and called my wife.

'Darling don't cook anything tonight. We are going to celebrate.'

'What! Longest marrow?' she said, clearly pleased with my success.

'Longest? No, I'm afraid I did not win that competition.'

'Really?'

'Yes, Best on Show. That's why I can take you out this evening.'

That evening at Bruno's restaurant, I asked for the stuffed marrow choice. It arrived looking like a courgette on the cusp of adolescence. But with its cargo of minced meat and mashed sweet potato, it certainly tasted good. I like my marrows.

I woke with a smile on my face. My wife asked me had I been dreaming again. I nodded.

'We are eating out tonight,' I said.

'What in lock-down?' she replied with a puzzled looking face.

'Oh well, let me go shopping. I'll make tonight's dinner. Do you fancy a marrow for tea?'

'Just a marrow?' she enquired.

Dream 10: Through The Eyes Of The Blind

This dream is based on reality during Christmas 1962. In alternative years my younger cousins and their parents came from Scotstoun in the west end of Glasgow to the Shawlands Old Parish Church Manse on Boxing Day where our family lived. I was aged 12, my sister 14, my brother aged 6 and my three Glasgow west-end cousins were, blind Brian aged 10, Dorothy 8, and Douglas 6. All the children sat near a roaring fire.

Midway through the afternoon, my father announced he had to fulfil an engagement at the Victoria Hospital, where he was the chaplain. I knew the plan was afoot. He waved goodbye to us all. My older sister was in on the secret too and we were told not to inform our cousins. Accordingly, it was no surprise to us that half an hour later we heard bells. Santa's reindeers were arriving at the manse. The younger children were besides their selves in excitement as they heard Santa coming upstairs to the lounge. The door opened and sure enough Santa Claus appeared in his red and white attire, black boots and a white beard to be proud to wear and be disguised. He arrived with a large brown sack over his shoulder.

Santa checked he was at the right house by asking each child their name. Dorothy informed Santa that her older brother was blind, but he was hearing every word.

Santa read each child's name and Dorothy, Miller, Joan, Bruce, Dorothy and Douglas came to Santa and received their Christmas present.

'Now that leaves just one present left. There's only one parcel left in my sack.' Santa lifted it out and asked, 'It's for Brian. Now where is Brian?'

Dorothy led her blind brother to Santa, and he received his present. However polite Brian just had to give his thanks.

'Thank you, Uncle Jim,' he said.

'No, no that's Santa, Brian. Not Uncle Jim,' explained Dorothy immediately and with concern not to offend Santa.

Brian took on board what Dorothy had said. But before returning to his place by the fire, he spoke once more to Santa.

'Thank you, Uncle Jim, for my present.'

Dream 11: A Spaceship Incident

I recall being in a spaceship. How I got there or why I was in the craft, I really can't explain. There was a crew of five. There were two Russians, one Chinese astronaut and an American and me. We all spoke English, enough to be understood, with heavy national accents. We were returning from a visit to Jupiter. We had circled one of the planet's moons, that being Callisto. Recordings had been penned into folders.

The flight was all in order until a rattling sound was heard. Worried looks came across the faces of the crew. The rattling became a shudder, and it was reported that one of the rockets had failed to ignite. Another rocket failed moments later and so the spacecraft was left with only one rocket to enable it to return to earth. It meant a longer and slower decent and this was communicated to Cape Canaveral. It also meant the planned re-entry into the Pacific Ocean could not be guaranteed. We all looked worried. Our food stocks were low, but our drinking water was available in good supply.

We entered the Earth's atmosphere and I saw the blue Pacific Ocean disappear and be replaced by dry land. I was told we would crash land in Southern Nevada in the Mojave Desert. We all looked at each other and saw death on our faces.

The ground became larger as we descended. Oleg thought he could try a controlled crash landing and heads shook their agreement, as no one had any better solution.

Then we braced ourselves for impact. My body shook. We had reached land, but our speed was still more than 500 mph. I heard branches breaking and stones hit the fuselage as we slid along the desert. Then we eventually came to a halt. We opened the hatch and realised there was a drop of twelve feet to the ground. I noticed the crash had damaged the water tank and it was spilling onto the arid land. We threw out pillows and blankets so that we could land on them but there was a rush as smoke could be detected coming from the damaged craft. It might go up in flames at any moment. We all jumped out within a minute. The American broke his ankle and was not only in pain, but he could not move away from the craft. Oleg banged his head on landing and was knocked out. The other Russian stayed behind in partial shade to attend to the injured and I started to walk to get help. I had walked for four minutes when I heard a loud explosion. The spacecraft had disintegrated. I knew immediately that the two Russians and the American could not have survived that explosion.

Where was the Chinese astronaut? He was nowhere to be seen. Perhaps he was a victim too. I walked back towards the smouldering spacecraft. Then I heard the sound of an approaching helicopter. It landed and I went to board it. Another helicopter arrived and I was told it would recover the dead. I was strapped into a seat and next to me was the Chinese colleague. I thumped his knee to indicate we had survived. And I had survived. I woke shortly afterwards. My body still tense from the experience.

Dream 12: 9/11

This is a dream of my friend Catherine Czerkawska. One I thought I should share with you as many of us can identify with certain moments.

Catherine Czerkawska is a well-known Scottish author who has provided an interesting dream about fact. She is a novelist, historian, and experienced professional playwright with the BBC. She lives in rural south Ayrshire:

‘OK - here's my dream. Nightmare really and a bit spooky’, writes author Catherine.

‘The night before 11th September 2001, I had one of the most appalling nightmares I've ever had.

I was in the middle of some catastrophe and was trying to escape. People were screaming, and dust and chunks of masonry were raining down from the sky.

I remember running and trying to take shelter from it all, underneath some kind of structure that we thought might protect us. Anything to get away from whatever was falling.

I woke up in a cold sweat - it was such a horrible dream that I told my husband, Alan, about it. It stayed with me all morning, and coloured my day, the way dreams like that do.

Then, in the afternoon, a friend phoned us and said, “Switch on your television. There's something happening at the twin towers ... “

If I hadn't told Alan about it, I don't think anyone would have believed me - but he will vouch for what I told him. It gave him such a frisson too.

Later on, I believe, some research was done - and many people seem to have had similar dreams - more than could be accounted for by 'coincidence'.

It was such a graphic and particular dream, as well, with nothing to account for it. I hadn't been watching any disaster movies or anything like that!”

The final entry is not a dream. It is a poem about a dream.

The Heron's Dream

A heron on the river Nith
Was lonely in November
His mate was nowhere to be found
Because he couldn't remember.

It's not just folk who have bad days
When everything's forgotten
All creatures are the same as us
And think it's really rotten.
Now I've provoked a truth not known
Well, hardly ever said
Because us folks unlike the fauna
Are just more widely read.
And as our dreams are often dreamt
Does the heron not dream too?
I suspect the fauna dream as well
Like cats and dogs, don't you?

The End

Printed in Great Britain
by Amazon

80561247R00109